Found Wanting

Sean H. Fitzmorris

This book is dedicated to my father, Norris, who encouraged me to become an EMT, and my wife Grainne who stuck with me through it all. And of course, to all the current and past heroes at New Orleans EMS, who work so hard at their job every day, unacknowledged and unthanked, risking themselves to save others. Thank you, guys. You're the best.

Acknowledgements:

Thanks to Tommy Evans, fellow EMT and death investigator for help with the forensic technical details.

To Monique and Mooney for help with character names.

To Jon and Sean for plot ideas.

To Mark for reading my drafts and encouraging me to continue.

To the entire staff at New Orleans EMS and every emergency room in New Orleans for their inspiration, stories and encouragement. You were family away from my family, my home away from home.

Chapter 1

He wiped his forehead; sweat had collected under his cap. The late summer sun burned down onto the concrete of Tulane's Emergency Department ambulance ramp, evaporating the recent afternoon rainfall into a citywide sauna. He took a moment before getting around to cleaning the back of the truck, staring at the mess he had made. Plastic wrappers, needles and syringes were strewn all over. He normally tried to keep trash in the trash can, but once in a while it felt good to make it look like he had been working. *'First things first,'* Marc thought. Cleaning up the back of the ambulance was his therapy after a code. Dirty needles were first to be picked up; he didn't want to stab himself with a sharp full of his homeless patient's hepatitis-laden blood. He pulled out the empty vial of potassium chloride from his pocket and pushed that into the sharps container too. Then he set about picking up all the Epinephrine and Atropine syringes and the paper and plastic trash before going back into the emergency room to finish his run report describing the cardiac arrest he had just brought in - a homeless drunk who had found his way into the back of Marc's ambulance more than a few times from his frequent drinking binges. The homeless guy, David, was a "frequent flier." EMS was summoned for him by the police and so-called good Samaritans almost daily for David passed out on a street or bloody from a fall or vomiting from his chronic hepatitis or just looking generally wretched. David was dead now. The nurses and doctors in the emergency room were working now to revive him in the hopes that soon David would be able to walk out of the hospital and resume his life of dependency on the kindness of others, and the profits of that kindness would be used to fuel his first post-cardiac arrest drinking binge. Marc, however, knew that David was not going to be coming back from the dead.

Later on that week Marc was back on duty. His patient tried to make eye contact as the truck bumped along North Claiborne. At one particularly abyssal pothole, the patient tried to stifle a scream but was less than successful. Marc noticed the patient's ruined leg flexing in the traction splint as the truck smacked every bump in the road. In his mind he could visualize the sharp bone fragments tearing through muscle and nerve tissue in exactly the way they shouldn't be torn through. *'That's gotta hurt,'* Marc thought. "Gimme a second, buddy, I have something that will help you for the ride." The young man on the spineboard looked hopefully at him; he was trying to be stoic, but Marc could see him struggling to hold back tears of pain. He knew it was bad enough for a seventeen year-old to have such a painful injury; the kid shouldn't have to be made to cry in front of a stranger as well.

"Try and take it easy!" he shouted to his partner up front in the driver's seat. He dug into his pocket and pulled out a small ampule from the case he carried, drew the med into a syringe and injected it into the patient's IV line. Moments later the patient's grimace relaxed a little, the tears receded. Marc carefully watched the EKG monitor and pulse oximetry. The boy's heartbeat slowed. The drug was having its effect.

"What did you give me?" he asked in a slightly drowsy voice.

"Fentanyl. It's a pain med that'll help you get through my partner's rough driving."

"Oh man, thank you!"

"No problem, man. You looked like you needed it." Marc gave a little smile to the patient, made sure the vital signs were OK, and continued his documentation.

At the hospital, Marc got his run report signed and wished the emergency room staff a good day; "I hope I don't see you again," he said, only half joking.

"Same here!" hollered the charge nurse, a pretty young thing with auburn hair, green eyes, big home-grown boobs and just enough makeup to accentuate the fact that she didn't need any makeup to be beautiful.

Marc walked out of the ER doors into the New Orleans heat and threw his clipboard into the ambulance, sat on the back bumper and lit up a cigarette. His partner, Brian, was finishing cleaning the ambulance, changing the linen on the stretcher and wiping up the specks of blood that had made it onto the floor.

"That was a pretty good call, huh?" Brian asked.

"That call? He'll be fine. Just a broken leg. All part of being a kid," Marc replied. Brian was a green EMT-Basic, on the streets for less than six months. *'He thinks every call is a good call. FNG.''*

"I've just never seen a bone poking out the skin like that," Brian contemplated. Their patient had been a seventeen-year-old boy, showing off on his new dirt bike for his buddies. He had hit the accelerator instead of letting it go and roared out of the empty lot into traffic, hitting a passing car broadside. His leg had gotten caught on the handlebars as he was ejected, fracturing the femur. The jagged bone edges had ripped through the skin, creating an open fracture. The kid would probably need surgery. Marc had already nearly forgotten the call. Brian would be talking about it for days. "I thought it was pretty cool," Brian affirmed.

Marc grunted noncommittally. "Let's try to find something to eat," he said with more enthusiasm.

Halfway to the nearest Subway, dispatch gave them a call. Canal and Royal Street. "Man down." Another drunk. "Shit!" Marc muttered, throwing the clipboard onto the dash. It was another regular. Aaron Sparrowhawk. How an American Indian got a Jewish first name was beyond Marc. Aaron was not only a drunk, but a crack abuser as well. He always had his Medicaid card and Louisiana Purchase card, the electronic version of food stamps. The Louisiana Purchase card could also be used, at taxpayers' expense, to withdraw cash to be used at one's friendly neighborhood drug dealer or liquor merchant. On this occasion, Marc and Brian found Aaron sitting in the middle of the sidewalk. He was wearing the same hospital paper scrub shirt and filthy jeans he had been in for weeks. He was soaked in his own urine and reeked of feces and alcohol, much like the last dozen times Marc had picked him up. He was so drunk he could barely slur anything approximating words. Brian and Marc hauled him off the ground by his arms & legs and plopped him onto the stretcher. Marc didn't need Aaron to give him any information; he already had Aaron's name, birthdate and social security number pasted inside his clipboard for occasions just like this one. Brian obtained vital signs and asked, "Do you want me to start an IV?"

Marc thought about the question. Each time he had picked Aaron up he had tried to learn more about him, to see if there were any redeeming qualities about the man. Aaron's mother was a prostitute; his father was serving a life sentence for murder in Arizona. He had sired two children by different women and had no contact with either woman since learning that they were pregnant. He had never had a job; his income had come from either welfare or stealing. He never used the money to buy food; he would instead eat whatever homeless shelters were serving or pick stuff out of a restaurant's dumpster. All the money was used for crack and alcohol. The closest thing to a redeeming quality Marc had found was when Aaron had once said "I *never* use heroin, though."

"No, that's OK, just gimme a ride to University," Marc instructed Brian. Brian hopped in the front seat and began to drive, leaving Marc and the now snoring Aaron alone in the back. As he scribbled his run report, Marc pondered David's fate a few days earlier, the homeless guy who suffered a "cardiac arrest" on the way to the hospital. Marc wondered how long it would be before Aaron suffered the same fate. Not today, though. It was too soon after David. But one day, not too far in the future, it was coming. Marc would make sure of it.

Chapter 2

"How long's it been?" Marc asked over his radio.

"You've been working it for fifteen minutes," came back the reply from dispatch.

'Five more minutes' he thought to himself. "Let's go with another Epi," he told Brian. Marc kept squeezing the Ambu bag to ventilate the patient through the endotracheal tube he had placed thirteen minutes earlier. The fireman continued pumping on the old lady's chest, which moved easily since the initial chest compressions had broken the ribs attaching the sternum. Marc had given pretty much all the drugs he could give to restore a heartbeat to the woman; the Epinephrine he had asked for was the fifth he would give to her. If all the other drugs hadn't made a difference in the flat line that the EKG monitor showed, this last one likely wouldn't either. But he was required to spend twenty minutes performing CPR and advanced cardiac life support before asking the medical control physician to pronounce the patient officially dead. And there were sometimes those moments that hovered between triumph and tragedy when the patient would regain a pulse nineteen minutes into the code. Those were the most difficult scenes. When that happened, there was a tiny thrill Marc would feel that his efforts were successful, but there was an even greater feeling of pity for the patient and the family. After nineteen minutes of anoxia, the brain is pretty much dead. The heart might be restarted, but of course a heart will beat even if it is removed from the body. CPR provides a poor substitute for a real heartbeat. Those patients who regained a heartbeat so long after clinical death would never walk out of the hospital; rather, they would spend their last few hours or days vegetating on a ventilator in some ICU, brain dead, with their family clinging to some false hope that they would wake up and be fine like in some

television melodrama.

"Fifth Epi in!" Brian announced as he pushed the med into the intraosseous line. *'Not much to do now but wait,'* Marc thought. The fireman continued chest compressions; Marc kept up the rhythmic squeezing of the Ambu bag. Brian scoped around for something to do, then began picking up the discarded trash around the old lady's bedroom. After a few minutes had ticked by, Marc rechecked the EKG monitor.

"Stop compressions," he said quietly to the fireman. He sat back, taking a break from the exhausting workout. Marc hit the print button on the monitor. The printout had only a thin, straight black line with no waves, bumps or any other indication of electrical activity in the woman's heart. He keyed up the radio and asked for the physician on the other end. "I'm on scene with a seventy year-old female, found down ten minutes prior to our arrival, unresponsive and apneic, asystole in all leads. History of hypertension, diabetes and two MI's. We got her intubated; got an IO on her. We've given her five Epi's, three Atropines, two milligrams Narcan, and an amp of dextrose and bicarb. After twenty minutes of CPR, she's still in asystole in all leads; calling for DNR."

The doctor responded, repeating back the sermon Marc had described, followed by "Ten-four, DNR is granted, time of death sixteen thirty-three."

And the old lady was dead.

"You got this, man?" Marc asked Brian. "I'm gonna go talk to the family. I have a feeling it oughta be entertaining."

"Yep," Brian said cheerfully as he continued picking up the waste from the floor and repacking the equipment to be put back into the ambulance. Brian loved working cardiac arrests and no task was too menial.

Marc opened the bedroom door and met the anxious family members in the hallway. "I'm very sorry, but we did everything possible, the same as she would have gotten in the hospital, but despite it all, she's died."

One or two of the family remained composed and resigned

themselves to the news. The other seven or eight family members began, as Marc had expected, to howl and shout and throw themselves against walls and furniture. "Oh lawd Jesus!" "Mama, no, you cain't leave me!" "Aw my God, aaaaaaahhhhh!" came the usual required shrieks and bellows. Marc felt sorry for the family, but *'is all this really necessary?'* he thought to himself. He observed the mounting hysteria in the front room; as folks continued rolling on the floor and hurling themselves at various objects he decided to seclude himself back in the bedroom with Brian and the firemen, where it would be safer. Marc locked the bedroom door and asked for dispatch to make sure the police were on their way to help control the scene. All six of the first responders exchanged silent glances at one another over the dead body as they listened to the ongoing ruckus in the rest of the house. After a few minutes they heard police dispatchers crackling over a radio in the other room and the howls had diminished to moans and cries. The sound of shouting and family members being pitched against furniture stopped. Marc opened the door and headed to the ambulance to write his report, pausing to say, "I'm so sorry for your loss," to the man who had earlier seemed least emotional of the crowd.

Marc sat on the back of the ambulance with his clipboard and a cigarette and began writing down the details of the scene. Halfway through, the least emotional man walked up to him with a little girl of about seven or eight in tow; she was wearing a bright pink frilly dress and lots of sparkly barrettes. The man said to Marc "Thank you for trying to help my mama; I'm sure you did your best." Before Marc could reply, the little girl chimed in too: "Thank you for trying to save my grandma, mister. You did all you could, but I know she's in a better place now."

Marc gasped silently to himself and did his best to choke down a little sob. He pulled the girl to himself and gave her a hug, a tear in both her eye and his. "You're welcome, darling. I'm so sorry I couldn't do more." His voice cracked a little as he said it. The girl gave him a sad smile and walked off hand in hand with her father. Marc quickly reviewed the scene in his head. He wasn't lying; he really had done all he could to save the girl's grandmother. Everyone dies, though, and no amount of medication or CPR can change that.

"Dispatch, you can clear me off this with a signal twenty-nine," he said over his radio. He spent the next half hour silently writing the rest of his report and thinking about the little girl, as Brian drove across town to wait for their next call. Marc hated it when he got choked up over a scene. *'You'd think after seeing a million deaths and murders and suicides that I wouldn't care anymore,'* he berated himself. But sometimes he did care, and another small voice berated him in another way, *'It proves you're human, after all.'*

'Damn it.'

His shift wore on. He and Brian responded to a motor vehicle accident with two patients, a diabetic who woke up with some IV dextrose and refused transport, a heroine addict overdosed, an old man feeling weak, a female who had gotten punched by another girl... a typical shift. At eleven PM, an hour before his shift was scheduled to be over, they got a call at Central Lockup for a man having chest pains. "You know this is utter bullshit, don't you?" he warned Brian.

"You mean a handcuff-induced heart attack?" Brian responded, chuckling out loud.

"You're a smart kid."

They pulled into the sprawling prison complex, waiting for the gates to open and close in the right order. A police officer shined his flashlight at them, motioning them to his location at the jailhouse door. From the ambulance, Marc could see a white guy about fifty years old sitting on a bench, alternately holding his chest and mouthing off to the cop. As he and Brian approached with the stretcher and equipment in tow, he could hear what the guy was hollering: "...I'm dyin' here and you tryna put me in jail... sue your ass... I'm dyin'..." And so on.

"For someone who's dying, you sure have a lot of energy," Brian said to the inmate. Marc smiled at Brian's spunk. For being such a new kid on the block, he was getting the hang of dealing with bullshit rather quickly.

Marc spoke up, "Don't tell me; let me guess. You got

arrested and then developed chest pains, right? So instead of jail you need to go to the hospital, right?"

"Yeah, man, that's exactly what happened. And this asshole cop is giving me shit about it! Says I ain't having no heart attack!" An almost visible cloud of alcohol fumes hovered around the man.

Marc turned to the police officer. "Isn't it amazing how people are never concerned about their health problems until they're drunk?"

"Or under arrest?" the officer replied, likewise knowing full well that the drunk was using his "chest pains" as a ploy to try to get out of going to jail.

Brian wasn't fooled either. He immediately hooked up the monitor to the drunk arrestee and ran a twelve lead EKG. "Looks fine to me! No heart attack here," he said, handing the strip to Marc.

Marc studied it for a minute. "Your EKG looks better than mine."

This wasn't the drunk's first time playing this game either. "I don't care; I'm still having chest pain and I need to go to the hospital! I'm dying!" he insisted. He knew as well as Marc, Brian and the policeman that he couldn't be refused treatment, and the ambulance would have to take him to the hospital.

"Fine, get on the stretcher," Marc ordered the guy. He and Brian rolled him to the ambulance. When they were out of earshot of the policeman, the man spoke to Brian, "Once the cops get tired of waiting for me at the hospital, they'll just give me a summons and cut me loose! You know what kind of food they got at the hospital tonight?" Brian shook his head. Marc didn't waste any effort looking more disgusted; they all knew that this was the objective of the whole game, after all. Marc was merely surprised that his patient had stated it so blatantly.

After loading him into the unit, Marc left Brian to start the paperwork and went back to the cop to ask what he had arrested the guy for in the first place.

"Public drunkenness, disorderly conduct and trespassing. Oh, and of course, soliciting sex from a nine year-old at McDonald's. Yeah, he's going to jail; he's not getting any summons, no matter how long it takes at the hospital."

Marc raised his eyebrows. "Soliciting sex from a nine year-old?"

"Yep," the cop verified.

The wheels in Marc's head started turning. *'Really?'* He climbed into the unit with the patient, gave him an aspirin and a squirt of nitroglycerine spray under his tongue, then started an IV in the drunk guy's left arm. The whole time Marc was pondering if this would be a candidate for his special form of therapy. This drunk was obviously useless to society. He had been in and out of jail so many times that he not only knew the game of asking for an ambulance when arrested, but was bold enough to speak of it openly to the EMT's. The address he had given was 843 Camp Street, the Ozanam Inn, a shelter for homeless men, or men who had gotten kicked out from whatever friends' house they had been crashing. Not only that, but this guy was preying upon little girls, or boys, or both. The one he had been arrested for soliciting was certainly not his first; it was just the latest victim he had gotten caught at.

He told Brian "I'm ready to go."

Brian jumped out the back and got into the driver's seat and began heading to University Hospital. The patient had been going on talking the entire time, varying his conversation between how his chest hurt and how he was "dying" and asking for something to eat and congratulating himself on his successful effort to get out of jail.

The more Marc listened, the more he was determined to make this ambulance trip the last drain on society this man would ever make. He didn't have much time; University was only a half-mile from the jail. As the ambulance bumped down Tulane Avenue, Marc reached into the bag containing all the medications they carried. He pulled out a prefilled syringe of calcium chloride. A gram would be sufficient. Calcium chloride is supposed to be administered very slowly. If pushed rapidly, the positively charged calcium ions in the bloodstream would neutralize the natural electrical conduction of the cells. Normally, positively charged potassium and calcium from the inside of the heart cells would switch places with the negatively charged sodium on the outside of the cells, then move back in. This ebb and flow of electrolytes was what stimulated the cells to contract and relax, resulting in a heartbeat. But flooding the heart with positive ions in the bloodstream would cause this process to stop. Marc visualized the cells in his mind, each positive calcium ion a tiny magnet. The calcium he would inject would repel the ions already in the cells, like two positive poles of magnets repelling each other. With nowhere for the ions to go, the ebb and flow would stop, as would the heart.

Marc preferred potassium chloride for this task, the same chemical that was used for lethal injections on death row, but it could be hard to come by. He had to quietly pocket vials of it that he found sitting around the emergency rooms and he hadn't been able to find any recently. Calcium would have to do. Both, however, were naturally occurring chemicals in the body; any autopsy would merely show hypercalcemia (or hyperkalemia, if potassium was used). Either diagnosis could easily be attributed to underlying medical problems such as drug use, renal failure or any number of conditions.

"I'm dyin'!" the drunk shouted as they passed over a bump. "Oh man! I'm dyin'!"

Marc opened the box containing the syringe. As he tore open the cardboard, another "I'm dyin'!" met his ears. He was disgusted with this individual. He contributed nothing to society; on the contrary, he sucked up resources, returning nothing. Marc envisioned rolling into University with the patient having suffered cardiac arrest after his calcium chloride injection. He saw a couple of difficulties with the idea and its possible consequences. First, the initial EKG showed no cardiac problems. Hypercalcemia usually shows up in some way on an EKG, as an unusual T-wave or a slow, ventricular rhythm. It would be difficult to attribute sudden death to hypercalcemia with such a normal EKG. Second, there would be an investigation within

NOPD regarding an arrestee's death, not to mention the media storm that would surely arise. The Times-Picayune and the public loved making NOPD look bad, no matter how incorrectly they got the story. The arresting cop, who had been simply doing his job, didn't need that kind of trouble, especially since the drunk had accused him of "giving him shit" for asking for an ambulance. Third, and most galling to Marc, was the man's insistence that he was dying. Marc did not want this individual to actually be right, since his existence was so obviously wrong.

As Marc put the drug back into the bag, he thought to himself *'I am not going let this asshole be right about "dying."'* He took comfort in the fact NOPD had assured him he *would* be going to jail, even more so when there were two more officers already waiting at University to keep an eye on the patient. Marc had let this one slide. As he moved the drunken sex offender onto a hospital stretcher, he reminded himself that there were plenty of others who deserved Marc's special therapy. You can't catch 'em all.

While finishing his run report, Marc happened to notice an unopened vial of potassium chloride sitting on a counter near the nurses' station. Later, after he had cleared from the call and left the hospital, one of the nurses who was mixing an IV drip for one of her patients thought to herself, *'I could have sworn I left that potassium right here. Hm. Oh well, someone must have thrown it away. I'll just call pharmacy for another.'*

Chapter 3

After he showered that night, he settled in on the couch flipping channels on the TV. He tried to pay attention to a travel show, but kept hearing the words of the little girl whose grandmother he had worked earlier. *"Thank you mister... I know she's in a better place now."* Like New Orleans' weather, which caused one hot, steamy day to blur into any other hot, steamy day, 911 calls tended to blur together. Endless cases of pain, vomiting, bleeding, seizures, drunks, overdoses, car accidents, falls and death eventually cause a person to forget the particular circumstances surrounding a particular symptom. Therefore, rarely did Marc think about work when he got home, but once in a while something stuck with him; a patient's expression, their words, an unusual injury... unique things that he would never forget. He had "war stories" just like any other EMT, but those were just stories; rarely would he remember the individuals involved. But sometimes there was an individual that he knew he would always remember. The granddaughter in the pink dress with the sparkly barrettes was going to be one of them. She and Marc had shared a brief moment on the girl's worst day, and that snapshot of her life was what would stay with him forever. In his memory she would be the sad girl in the happy dress, trying not to cry - forever. Marc wondered how she would remember him. In her memory, would he be someone who had really tried to save her grandma's life? Or would he be just some guy sitting on an ambulance bumper with a clipboard and cigarette, going on about his shift as if nothing had happened? Both viewpoints would be true. Marc resigned himself to knowing that no matter how the girl thought of him, there was nothing he could change about it. He went to the kitchen and poured himself a full glass of bourbon. Later that night, Marc dreamed of sparkly barrettes.

They metamorphosed into sparkling butterflies and swarmed around his head, scintillating as they flew. As he smiled at them and reached out to catch one, they all dropped to the ground, dull and dead.

The next morning came too early. His shift started at ten in the morning. Marc dragged himself out of bed at nine, gulped down about a quart of water and took some Tylenol to nurse his hangover from last night. After a quick shower, he brushed his teeth and noticed the slight paunch that he had developed. *"I'm not 19 anymore,"* he though to himself, though he was still a tall, powerful, and he thought, good-looking man. He made a mental note to trim his increasingly walrus-like blonde mustache when he had the time. He Febreeze'd his uniform from yesterday, threw it on, and headed out the door to the station.

He spent the first hour of his shift uptown, dodging 911 calls, finding coffee and saying hello to the staff at Baptist Hospital, near the location in the city to which he had been assigned to cover. Finally he and Brian got a call for "chest pains." Naturally, it turned out to be nothing of the kind; whatever system dispatch used to triage calls didn't work. The woman with "chest pains" actually turned out to be in labor. They dropped her off at Touro and left to run more calls. They responded to a motor vehicle accident where nobody wanted to go to the hospital and a nine year-old having an allergic reaction, requiring Benadryl and Epinephrine. Then another "chest pains" out in New Orleans East.

The man to whom they were dispatched actually was having chest pains. Both Brian and Marc were surprised that dispatch had gotten the call right for a change. The patient was a sixty-one year-old man, living in a trailer park. He had been working on his friend's car when he started feeling "like an elephant's sitting on my chest." He was pale and clammy and had trouble getting up off the ground to sit on the stretcher.

'This dude is sick,' Marc thought. Brian hooked up the EKG and ran a printout. It looked like he was having the beginnings of a heart attack. Marc told him so, and he replied, "Man, this is a hell of a way to spend my day off." He grimaced in pain. "I work construction and I hurt myself all the time; nothing bothers me. But this... man, this is killing me!"

"I'm ready to go," Marc told Brian after having been on scene for only seven minutes. Marc would complete the rest of the patient's care en route to the hospital. As they bumped out of the gravel road of the trailer park, Marc stuck the IV in, gave him Nitroglycerine, aspirin and two milligrams of Morphine. A few minutes later, none of the drugs had had any effect. Marc glanced at the monitor and noticed that the waves looked a little different than they had a few minutes earlier. He reached over the man on the stretcher to print out another EKG. As he looked closer at the monitor, he saw that what had started off as barely indicative of a heart attack was now a textbook example of one. The electrical complexes now showed waves called "tombstones." They were called that for two reasons - one, they were shaped like a tombstone on the printout and two, they usually indicated the fate of the patient.

While Marc was hovering over the stretcher studying the EKG, the patient grabbed Marc's hand and held on tight. "Man, I don't think I'm gonna make it. I feel like... like my heart doesn't have any strength. I think I'm gonna die," he said almost matter-of-factly. Marc didn't want to say *'I think you're right.'* Instead he just let the man hold his hand. There was nothing else Marc could do for the progressing heart attack, other than get to the hospital. He held the patient's hand until they pulled up onto the hospital ramp.

As they walked into the doors, Marc silently mouthed to the physician waiting there *'He's going to code.'* Ten minutes later, he did. The ER staff was able to restore the man's heartbeat after two defibrillation attempts. A few minutes after that, he was rolled up to the cath lab where the cardiologist would try to open up the blocked arteries in the man's heart.

"You saved his life," said both Dr. Harlow and Mignon, the charge nurse.

Marc said, "Did I? He's not doing too hot, you know."

"He's alive. You got him here and gave him a chance."

Marc pondered that for a minute. If it had been ten minutes later before the man called 911 or Marc and Brian had delayed on scene a little longer, there was no question the man would have died. Marc really had saved his life. It wasn't the first time Marc had saved anyone's life, but it was rare that people actually put it in those terms, especially ER doctors and nurses. It made Marc feel good. The patient may have been a bit rough around the edges, but he was polite, and he had a job. He had also been working on someone else's car, helping out his friends. The man was a productive member of society, actually giving into the system. Marc didn't care if the guy was scruffy or lived in a trailer in a bad part of town. His patient actually contributed something to the world, and didn't just suck up resources like a tick on the skin of civilization. Marc had saved that life, or at least given him a chance. That was when Marc loved his job.

"Strong work," Marc complimented Brian who was waiting at the bottom of the ramp after cleaning up the back of the unit.

"I didn't do much; I just drove here," he protested.

"Getting here is exactly what that guy needed. There's nothing I can do for an MI in the back of the truck, other than say 'yep, you're having an MI.' The meds don't do anything for an actual heart attack. Thanks for not giving me shit when I said it was time to go. We were only on scene for seven minutes. With a patient like that, you treat 'em with diesel."

"I guess so." Brian paused. "Thanks, man," he said as he tried to hold back a smile.

They ran a few more calls - a sprained ankle, a panic attack, another woman in labor. Nothing that actually needed an ambulance, which was typical of most EMS calls in New Orleans. Day turned to night and the tourists began to flood the French Quarter. Several calls involving drunks came out over the radio for other units. The ambulances responded to drunks who fell, drunks who got into fights, drunks who wrecked their cars, drunks who had too much to drink. Eventually Marc and Brian got their drunk call - a "man down" at Canal and Royal, Aaron Sparrowhawk's usual hangout. There was a liquor store there that sold rotgut booze cheap enough that the bums on the street could afford it. Brian guided the ambulance to the corner and pointed out their target to Marc. Aaron was passed out in the gutter, clutching an empty pint of Skol vodka.

NOPD's Homeless Assistance team was there too. Marc wasn't sure what they did, other than bring the homeless to shelters. The middle-aged blonde woman, Margie, was on duty with their crew. Brian went back to the unit to get the stretcher while Margie talked to Marc. "You know we found him a place to stay, not in a shelter. The judge even ordered him into the apartment," Margie explained.

"I didn't know judges could order you into a residence," Marc replied.

"Yes, and we got him into rehab for his substance abuse. He never went to rehab and stayed in the apartment for five days before he was back out on the streets. He *wants* to live on the streets and drink and smoke crack all day. Even found a family member in Arizona to see if they could help. The family wanted nothing to do with him."

"I can't blame them," Marc said quite honestly to Margie. He looked down at Aaron and noticed some blood staining the detritus in the gutter in which he was lying. It was coming from a fresh laceration on his scalp, sustained when he fell against the curb in his current drunken stupor. "He's gonna need a board and collar," he said flatly to Brian. Marc got the cervical collar and spineboard out of the truck, laid it on the street behind Aaron's back and rolled him onto it. He wrapped the cervical collar around Aaron's neck and velcroed it into place to immobilize the spine. As he and Brian secured the straps on the board, they both tried to keep as much distance as possible between their noses and Aaron, as his usual body-odor/urine/feces/alcohol smell mixed with the indescribably noxious effluent that collected in the gutters of the French Quarter and now dripped from his hair and clothes.

Marc glanced at Margie. "So this is how he wants to live," he commented in a low, disappointed voice.

In the back of the truck, Brian read off Aaron's pulse and

blood pressure. "Heart rate one-twelve, blood pressure two-ten over a hundred and forty. Aaron was still passed out, but he'd wake up and slur a bit when Brian rubbed a couple of knuckles on Aaron's sternum. His astronomical blood pressure was usual for him; few of the EMT's at the service had seen it much lower than it was now. The clerk at the rotgut store had mentioned that the pint Aaron had been clutching was the second one he'd had in two hours.

Brian attached the EKG electrodes. "Sinus tach," he said to Marc.

'The kid may be green, but he's catching on fast,' Marc thought. "Not bad," he said. "Are you in paramedic class?"

"Not yet, but I start soon and I'm trying to get a head start studying EKG's."

"Well, you want to try for an IV on our friend here?" Marc offered.

Brian started the IV with only one attempt. He hooked up the line of saline to the catheter and secured it, checked Aaron's glucose level from the blood in the needle. "One fifty-two," he said. "Where are we going?"

"I don't know, all the hospitals are full up," Marc replied, exasperated at the thought. The last thing he wanted was to have to sit and wait for a bed at some ER with Aaron for an hour or two inhaling the toxic fumes emanating from him.

"He's got a band from EJ on; wanna go there?" Brian asked.

Marc looked down at the patient's right wrist. Sure enough, there was a hospital band from East Jefferson Hospital, left on from his last visit two days ago, according to the date on the band. "Sounds like a plan to me. If they didn't want him to come back then they should have cut off the band when they discharged him last time."

As Brian climbed out of the back to get into the driver's seat, Marc paused from writing his report and looked intently at Aaron. *'This is exactly the kind of person that does not need to be here. Or anywhere. At all.'* Marc thought carefully about the circumstances. *'It's been over a month since David. Sparrowhawk's blood pressure is through the roof, as usual. He has a head injury already, along with at least two pints of vodka and God knows how much crack. He has a fucked up EKG too; normal for him, but who's gonna complain? I have a good fifteen or twenty minutes to the hospital. Even his own family wants nothing to do with him. This guy has always been and always will be a drain on the rest of the world and to top it all off, he reeks worse than a landfill by his own choice.'*

Marc's mind was made up.

Whenever he rendered this service to patients, he had several options open to him on exactly what to do. As he contemplated his choices, inevitably the words and voice of the Wicked Witch of the West would screech through his mind: *"The only question is how to do it? These things must be done delicately, or you'll hurt the spell!"* Marc, though, didn't wish to terrorize his "Dorothy" lying on the stretcher; Sparrowhawk's end would be enough. He opened up the bag with all the medical equipment and fished out the case containing the drugs, removing three ampules of Epinephrine of 1:1000 concentration. The highly concentrated Epi was normally used in tiny doses and injected subcutaneously for allergic reactions. It was the chemical equivalent of adrenaline, raising pulse and blood pressure. By injecting the entire three milligrams undiluted directly into Sparrowhawk's veins, it would raise his pulse and blood pressure to deadly levels.

Marc drew up the Epi into a syringe and waited till they were committed to the Interstate, so that East Jefferson, still ten or fifteen minutes away, would be considered their closest facility to transport what was about to become a critical patient, or if they did turn around, the hospitals in town would still have the same, long transport time.

Marc pushed the three milligrams of Epi into the IV. A moment later, the heart rate on the EKG monitor climbed from one hundred twelve to two hundred eighty. Marc checked Aaron's blood pressure. Three hundred over two hundred. The physiological changes wracking the patient caused him to wake up briefly and cry in pain. Marc imagined Aaron's anatomy. The blood vessels in his body would be weak, starved from nourishment by a steady diet of alcohol and crack cocaine. The body's cells needed proteins and vitamins to reproduce, and Aaron had denied them that for years. Inside his brain, where the largest amount of blood flowed at one time from the heart, the weakened vessels would begin to rupture. The tremendous pressure generated by the Epinephrine would cause the blood to rush out from the vessels into the space in the skull, creating intracranial pressure for which the brain was unable to compensate. At the same time, the cells in the heart were being overstimulated. The electrical impulses normally progress from one part of the heart to another and results in an orderly, rhythmic squeezing motion - a heartbeat. Aaron's though, was beating entirely too fast. Hearts that beat over about a hundred and sixty times a minute have a risk to destabilize into ventricular fibrillation, where impulses are generated irregularly from all over the heart, instead of from the normal pathways.

Aaron tried to look at Marc from the spineboard where his head was strapped. As the pressure from the bleeding inside his head rose to lethal levels, Aaron had a seizure, his body convulsing for a few minutes before relaxing in death. The EKG showed ventricular fibrillation, wavy lines with no pattern. Aaron was apneic, not breathing, turning blue. "He just coded!" Marc said to Brian up front.

"You want me to pull over and come help you?"

"No, I got it, you keep going. Tell dispatch."

Brian keyed up his radio to alert dispatch of the patient in cardiac arrest. Brian wasn't sure why they needed to know, neither was Marc, but they just wanted to know these things for some reason.

Marc attached the defibrillator pads to Sparrowhawk's chest, charged them and shocked. The wavy lines settled down into a straight, flat line. *'Great, that makes things much easier.'* He had been afraid that the defibrillation attempt might actually restore Sparrowhawk's pulse. Now, despite the Epinephrine, the pressure in his skull was stimulating the vagus nerve, which slows down the heart rate. In Aaron's case, it was slowed to nothing.

Marc got out his intubation gear. He guided the laryngoscope blade into Aaron's mouth till he could see the vocal cords and slipped the endotracheal tube between them. He filled the cuff with air so the tube would stay in place. The wire stylet that helped keep the tube's shape had a small cap on the end to hold it in place. The cap formed a cover and had to be removed before ventilating the patient. Marc left it in place. He placed the Ambu bag on Aaron's lap; he would need it later, but for the ride Aaron was getting no oxygen. Marc attached the carbon dioxide detector to the EKG monitor. It was designed to connect to the endotracheal tube and show when the patient had normal levels of CO_2, indicating a good intubation, or reduced levels, indicating a tube in the esophagus, rather than the trachea. Since Marc held the other end in his own mouth and breathed through it, the monitor was showing perfectly normal carbon dioxide exchange.

It was time for drugs. According to ACLS algorithms, since the patient was asystolic with no electrical activity, Epinephrine and Atropine were the first two drugs to use. Marc opened the prefilled syringes, squirted one Epi and one Atropine into the wheel well where the side door of the ambulance was and told Brian "First Epi and Atropine in!" Brian diligently informed dispatch.

Marc made sure to perform a few real chest compressions; he had to break a few ribs with compressions to make it appear that Sparrowhawk had been receiving CPR the entire time. Marc also thought it looked good to print an EKG strip with the telltale artifact of chest compressions. In addition, Brian couldn't see much of the back from his rearview mirror through the tiny window dividing the cab and patient compartment of the ambulance, but Marc made sure that it looked like he was doing CPR. After feeling the crack of a few popped ribs in Aaron's chest, Marc just sort of bounced up and down with his hands on Aaron's chest to make it look like CPR, but without the pressure required to generate blood flow, pausing to squirt more drugs into the wheel well.

As the ambulance pulled off the interstate onto Clearview Parkway, Marc retraced his steps. Aaron was intubated, with no pulse or respirations. He counted the drugs he had "administered," three Epi's, three Atropines and fifty milliequivalents of sodium bicarbonate. *'Good enough for a ten minute code,'* he thought. He ran another EKG strip. It still showed the flat line of death. He performed a few more chest compressions so the monitor would capture them in print, along with the perfect levels of carbon dioxide. The monitor didn't care where the gas was coming from, in this case Marc's own lungs, it only recorded what it found. Marc glanced at the capped tube extending into Aaron's airway. As they made the final turn to go up East Jefferson's ramp, Marc removed the cap from the ET tube and removed the stylet and attached the carbon dioxide monitor and the Ambu bag. He gave a few ventilations to blow off the carbon dioxide that had no doubt accumulated in the lungs.

Brian parked the truck and came around back to unload the patient. As they rolled the stretcher into the ER, Brian hopped up onto the rail and did CPR and let Marc push him and the stretcher, "codesurfing" as it was known in EMS. They moved him onto the hospital stretcher in the trauma room and Marc gave his official report of what happened. "We found him down with a head injury, plenty of alcohol on board. Initially his pressure was high, but that's usual for him. Halfway here, he coded; went into v-fib. He's had one defibrillation, three Epi's, three Atropines, an amp of bicarb, almost a liter of saline and he's got a seven point five ET tube. Been in asystole ever since the first defib."

"Okay, good job," said Dr. Ramirez, the ER physician on duty. "He looks familiar."

"Yeah, he's got an EJ armband from two days ago. That's why we came here; we figured you wanted him back."

"Oh yeah, I remember," Ramirez said. "He was drunk off his ass. Positive for cocaine too. Outstanding individual."

"Isn't he? It's the aroma that I'd like to bottle and sell. Filth cologne."

Ramirez snickered and turned to his new patient. "Go ahead with another Epi. What was his glucose?"

"One fifty-two," Marc answered. "Doc, I'm gonna go to my truck; I'll be back in a few." Marc went out onto the ramp and began cleaning the back of the truck. He made sure the ampules of 1:1000 Epi were disposed of in the sharps box. Then he set about his usual routine of cleaning up after a code, pondering his handiwork.

Sparrowhawk had had no heartbeat for at least ten minutes and no real CPR to generate blood flow to critical organs. He had received no oxygen through the tube in his throat. All the drugs to restart his heart had trickled out the drain in the bottom of the ambulance onto the interstate. This was enough to cause irreversible brain death, even if the emergency room staff was able to restore a heartbeat. In addition, the amount of swelling inside the skull was enough to ensure that Aaron Sparrowhawk would never be found down drunk again. The blight that was his existence had been brought to an end.

Marc smiled subtly to himself as he wrote his run report. His documentation would certainly not include the three milligrams of Epinephrine that had begun the cascade of events leading up to cardiac arrest. His report said simply that the patient went into ventricular fibrillation and later remained in asystole. Any autopsy would show brain hemorrhage that obviously led to death, no doubt caused by the head injury, and exacerbated by alcoholism, crack abuse and untreated hypertension. Aaron would be buried, or cremated, his funeral unattended and forgotten... pretty much the same way he lived his life.

As Marc sat on the bumper of the ambulance writing, another New Orleans EMS unit pulled up. Cindy was driving and came around to unload her patient. Her partner was Grace, who hopped out the back, waved to Marc and said "I heard you killed another one!"

Marc grinned at the irony of her joke. "Yep, sure did. Sparrowhawk. He's a goner."

"Oh my God," said Grace, "I thought he'd never die, that

boil on the butt of humanity! Strong work, sir!"

"Amen," replied Marc.

By the time Marc finished writing, Aaron had been pronounced dead. He got one of the nurses to sign his run report and left. It was the end of his shift, so he and Brian headed back to the station to wash the truck and restock supplies. He filled out his requisition form. Ricky, the guy who was working rescue tonight also had the responsibility to restock the bags. Ricky engaged Marc in the usual banter, never questioning the use of any of the meds he asked to be restocked, including the three 1:1000 Epi's. He happily sealed the bag and gave it back to Marc, wishing him a good night.

Marc thanked him and added "Oh, it's already been a good night."

Chapter 4

Days later, Marc was back at work. He clocked in, put his gear in the truck and turned on his radio. Even before he let dispatch know that he and Brian were in service, they were looking for him on the radio to take one of the calls that were holding. After he copied the information down, Marc turned to Brian and said "I hope this isn't the way this whole day is going to go. I don't feel well and don't have the patience for bullshit today."

"What's wrong? You sick?" Brian inquired.

"No, just tired. I've been busier on my last few days off working around the house than I am at work, and this day isn't starting out well, getting a call before we're even in service. Which means we're gonna be inundated with bullshit calls all day. Plus I think I'm a little hungover."

Brian nodded as he drove to the scene they had been sent to. It was a motor vehicle accident. Sizing up the scene, it looked like the female driver had gotten too close to the side of the road and banged a parked car - nothing major; a little fender and headlight damage. *'Hardly anything to this wreck, which means this bitch is gonna want to be transported,'* Marc predicted to himself.

He predicted accurately. As he and Brian approached the vehicle, there were people standing next to the car. Apparently the driver had called several of her friends to the scene beforehand. They performed their duty, screaming at Marc and Brian, insisting their friend was critically injured, telling them to 'hurry up.' The driver sat quietly in the car, calmly looking through her purse for something while her friends continued the hubbub on the street.

Brian spoke to the driver, "Are you hurt ma'am?"

"Mister, I feel like I'm burning up with fever."

Marc couldn't quite hear the conversation so he asked Brian to repeat what she had said. "She says she feels like she has a fever," Brian repeated clearly, rolling his eyes.

"Fever? We're called to a car crash and she says she has a fever? Seriously? Motor vehicle induced fever... just when I thought I'd heard it all." Marc laughed humorlessly, and asked the woman what was wrong with her himself.

"I feel like I'm coming down with a fever," she repeated. Noticing Marc's facial expression, she added "What?"

Marc realized his jaw was hanging open. "It's just that I've never had a patient involved in a car crash say their problem was a fever. Do you want us to take you to the hospital?"

The woman paused, as if that thought had never occurred to her, even though there was an ambulance, two EMT's and a half-dozen friends shouting about how "injured" she was, all within several feet of her immediate vicinity. "Yeah, I guess it'd be a good idea to go get checked out."

'Of course it would be,' Marc thought to himself. His wish for a minimum-bullshit day was already evaporating. He and Brian hauled out the stretcher, spineboard and cervical collar and got the patient out of the car and secured her to everything. As they were attaching all the straps and tape, Marc asked "Is anything wrong with you besides feeling like you have a fever? Like, did you hurt yourself in the accident?"

"No."

Marc closed his eyes for a moment to try to compose himself. He so badly wanted to shout at the woman about how much of a waste of time this was, how she's taking the ambulance out of service for the rest of the city for her non-issue, how his tax dollars were going to be spent to pay for this completely unnecessary ride and her subsequent ER visit, but he managed to hold his tongue. He occupied himself with paperwork and vital signs. Since her dire emergency was feeling like she had a fever, Marc checked her temperature. It was 98.6, exactly what every textbook on earth said it should be. "No fever," he informed her, doing his best to inflect as much contempt and disgust as he could into those two words, but simultaneously being cheery enough that the patient wouldn't file a complaint. To be written up for disciplinary action for this ridiculous scene was not worth the trouble.

At the hospital, Marc informed Sunny, the triage nurse, of the patient's information. "She got into an accident and felt like she has a fever."

"What?" Sunny asked, eyebrows raised.

"You heard me. I can't make this shit up," Marc replied.

"And did you check her temperature? Does she have a fever?"

"Nope. Ninety-eight point six."

Sunny paused, wondering what to put on the triage form for a chief complaint. "So what would you say is wrong with her?" she asked Marc, at a loss.

"Same thing I wrote on my report, 'I think I have a fever.' Quotation marks for patients' ridiculous complaints are my best friend." he replied.

"What a waste of time," Sunny muttered.

Brian piped up, his usually cheerful demeanor marred by the whole affair, "I couldn't have put it better myself."

A few minutes after they cleared from that call, they were sent to the Salvation Army homeless shelter for someone complaining of "leg swelling." The patient was waiting in the lobby. She was a forty-four year old woman, in apparently reasonably good health, though unkempt and smelly. Obviously she hadn't bathed in a week. She met them at the door, walking perfectly erect carrying a duffel bag and several plastic grocery bags, with no immediate indication of anything apparently wrong with her legs.

"I need to go to the hospital!" she commanded Brian and Marc before either medic had even had a chance to say hello.

"I take it you're the patient. What's going on with you today?" Marc asked, sarcasm only slightly apparent in his voice over her lack of manners.

The woman began rolling up her pants leg and barked "I got a rash on my leg. They said it was cellulitis. I need to go get antibiotics for it."

"Who said it was cellulitis?" Brian asked while inspecting the reddened area on her calf.

"The doctor. I went to the emergency room last week. They told me it was cellulitis."

Marc asked "Did you get a prescription for antibiotics?"

"Yeah, but I never got it filled," she said as she uncrumpled the prescription paper from her pocket. "I need to go back to the hospital."

"By ambulance? Where did you come from to get to the shelter here?" Marc said, feeling his impatience gnawing at his insides like a shark tearing up a seal.

"I walked here from the other shelter on Oretha Castle Haley."

Brian furrowed his brow at Marc, calculating the distance from that shelter to this one. "That's like two and a half miles," he informed everyone. "You know Baptist Hospital is, like, right there," he said, pointing over the fence at the huge hospital complex a block away. The street that the door of the shelter opened onto ran exactly one block until it dead-ended at the entrance to Baptist's emergency room. At certain times of the day, the Salvation Army shelter sat quite literally in the shadow of Baptist Hospital.

"So let me get this straight," Marc began. "You went to the doctor already for the same problem and didn't get your prescriptions filled. Then you walked two and a half miles to this shelter on the leg that has cellulitis. And now you called 911 for an ambulance to bring you exactly one block to the emergency room to be seen for the problem you've already been treated for? Am I leaving anything out?"

She fidgeted with her bags. "Well I didn't get my prescriptions filled 'cause I didn't have no money." As she repositioned her belongings, one of the plastic bags ripped, dropping two fresh, unopened packs of cigarettes onto the floor.

"No money, huh? Where do you get your free cigarettes? I smoke and would love to find a place that gives them away for free. Get in the truck," Marc ordered her, turning and heading back to the ambulance. The woman scrambled to pick up her cigarettes and catch up with Marc. Brian seatbelted her into the seat in the back of the truck. As Marc silently began his paperwork, he kept wishing he would have a legitimate reason to start an IV on the woman and a transport time longer than thirty seconds. She certainly met his preliminary criteria for his unique form of therapy. But this was the first time he had ever met her. He knew nothing about her background, other than she was currently homeless and obviously knew how to milk the system. *'But who knows? She may have a real family somewhere or some sort of contribution to society,'* Marc thought. Oddly, it seemed as if the woman sensed Marc's thoughts, for as the ambulance pulled onto the ramp, the woman spoke up, saying "I used to work here. My daughter did too up until Katrina."

Curious, Marc pursued the conversation, "You worked at Baptist?" *'Whaddya know, she actually had a job!'* he considered.

"Yeah, I worked in housekeeping. My daughter was a tech here and she was in nursing school when the hurricane hit. She moved to Atlanta and finished her nursing degree."

'Wow, so she actually was a productive citizen and it sounds like her daughter is too,' Marc pondered. He had found a redeeming quality about the woman. She may have been down on her luck now and mooching off welfare and the kindness of others, but at least she had earned it. She had paid taxes and held a job and raised a daughter who was apparently also a productive member of society. Marc didn't begrudge her the welfare she received or the Medicaid money that went to her healthcare. She had already contributed her part and had earned the right to use it, even though her usage of the ambulance today was still 911

abuse. *'But if I got rid of everybody who abused the ambulance, half the city would be gone,'* he considered.

As they walked towards the ER doors, Marc turned to her and said "I'm sorry if I seemed a little harsh on you. But you're obviously someone who can take care of yourself and I want to see you do that. You have the capability to be self-reliant; don't get sucked into the endless cycle of handouts and welfare. I know you can do better for yourself."

She looked inquisitively at Marc, but appeared to recognize that he was encouraging her to do better with her life, no longer scolding her for being a parasite. She wondered what she had done to change the paramedic's rather hostile demeanor during the thirty-second ride, but apparently chose not to pursue the question. Instead, as they walked into the doors, she asked one of the nurses nearby "Y'all got a vending machine in here? Where's the bathroom? I really gotta go."

Desiree, the nurse, pointed down the hall and the patient hurried off. "I'm pretty sure she can go to the waiting room," she informed Marc.

"Yeah. I thought so too," he answered. *'She doesn't deserve death, but she's still a pain in the ass,'* he concluded.

Chapter 5

As they pulled off the ramp, Brian exclaimed "Man, what a dirt bag! I never realized how many useless people there were in this world till I started this job. I wanted to work in the medical field because I always wanted to help people, but so many don't want any help; they just want handouts and for everyone else to do everything for them!"

"Yep," Marc agreed. "I was the same as you when I first started. But seeing all the scum of society everyday all day makes you a little... jaded. I've gotten to the point where I don't really care if these idiots live or die. It's great when you can make a real difference in someone's life, but those moments are few and far between."

Brian thought for a minute. "I don't think we've had a real patient in weeks! Other than that heart attack last week. And Sparrowhawk. Of course we didn't really make any difference with him, seeing as he's dead now."

Marc turned to the front, staring out the windshield. Brian thought Marc appeared oddly distracted at that moment. Eventually Marc replied, "Yeah, he needed to go."

'That's a weird way to put it,' Brian thought. "I don't think anyone will miss Sparrowhawk."

"Let's go get some coffee; I'm still tired," Marc suggested.

Just as they got their coffee, another call came out for "leg pain."

"This is gonna be another bullshit call," Marc commented flatly. He seemed to be doing a good job at deflating Brian's enthusiasm for picking up any and every patient, as Brian let out a long, drawn-out sigh.

"I have a feeling you're right," Brian replied.

At the house, the door was open and they walked in. The two medics found a swirl of family members in the front room. Some appeared to be arguing, a couple sat and stared at the TV blaring "The Price is Right" at full volume. After standing there in the house completely unnoticed for a full two minutes, one woman finally acknowledged their presence and pointed down the hallway of the shotgun house. "He's all the way in the back."

Brian asked Marc quietly, "Why are they always 'all the way in the back'?"

Marc muttered "I have no idea, other than to make it extra difficult for us to get them out. No one ever gets sick in the front room, or downstairs."

They passed a bedroom with a couple mattresses lying on the floor, about a half-dozen children sleeping on them. "Why aren't they in school? It's Thursday!" Brian again whispered.

"What, and get an education and maybe get out from this hovel? Gain an opportunity for a better life off welfare? Can't have that."

Brian was still shaking his head as they entered the patient's bedroom. There were three or four other female family members hovering around the bed. The man in the bed was dozing, and woke up as Marc said "Hey, sir! How are you? What's going on?"

Before the man could respond, one of the women spoke up, "It's his foot; I think it's infected."

Marc hated when bystanders didn't give the patients a chance to speak for themselves. He didn't turn to the woman who had spoken but continued to address the man. "How do you feel? What's wrong with your foot?"

The man began to say "I feel fi..."

"I TOLD YOU IT'S HIS FOOT THAT'S INFECTED!" the woman hollered at Marc.

"Ma'am, I heard you. But I have to ask the patient what's going on. I know he's having foot issues, but I need to know if he's in his right mind and oriented and so on," Marc replied with all the self-control he could muster.

The woman grunted and left the room. Marc began pulling the bed sheets off the man, saying "Okay, let's have a look at this foot of yours."

As he uncovered the man's feet, Brian gasped. His left foot looked pretty normal, dry skin and horny nails, not unusual for an elderly diabetic. The right foot, though, was far from normal. The skin was blackened, far blacker than the rest of the man's coffee complexion. It was not just dry, but desiccated, the shape of the bones of the foot clearly visible through the thin, beef-jerky skin. Marc touched it gently with a gloved hand to see if there was any pulse whatsoever. As his palm brushed against one of the dried toes, the remnants of the toenail simply fell off onto the bed. "Oh, my God." Marc rarely was astonished at the condition of patients, but even he had never seen a completely dead, mummified appendage attached to a living person.

"How long has it been like this?" Marc asked anyone in the room willing to respond.

The disgruntled woman stomped back into the room. "It's been like that for a while."

"Why haven't you brought him to the doctor? Why did you wait till it was like this to call the ambulance?"

"We just thought it would get better. We been praying for him to get better. We done had the minister out here a bunch of times to pray over him. And we been putting lotion on him."

Marc blinked, at a loss for words. He looked at Brian, who was still staring at the zombie-like foot. It was like a train wreck; he couldn't help but stare. Marc thought about what to say; a thousand different synonyms for "stupid," "ignorant" and "hopeless" flooded his mind. Finally he decided that simple words would be best for this crowd, preferably one-syllable words. He turned to the patient who, after all, was the one who had to carry the dead foot around. "Sir, your foot isn't infected. Your foot is dead. It's going to have to be cut off at the hospital."

The man wailed, "Oh Lord Jesus, no! My foot! I can't lose

my foot!" The family members also lost it, throwing their hands up in the air, asking for the Lord's help, crying and shrieking. Marc glanced at Brian. Brian whispered "How can this be a surprise?"

Marc shrugged and said, "Let's just get the stretcher in here."

They trundled the old man out of the house, navigating past the multitude of family and friends in the bedroom, front room and on the porch. Besides the ones watching TV, still enraptured by "The Price is Right," all seemed to be in varying states of panicky prayer at the announcement that the necrotic foot was dead. Brian wondered what the reaction would be when the rest of the old man eventually died.

At the hospital, Marc gave his report to the ER staff. All the nurses and doctors were as impressed at the condition of the foot as Brian and Marc had been. There was no question that it would have to be amputated. When Dr. Lovejoy asked why it had taken months, obviously, to do something about it, her jaw hung open when Marc informed her that prayer was probably not the best primary healthcare route to take.

"They just prayed? Did they think that he would just grow a new foot or something?" she asked, incredulous.

"Apparently so. Seeing as all six kids at the house weren't even in school, I doubt that education or knowledge of such things is high on their priority list. I'm just amazed he hasn't died of sepsis."

After they left the patient, Brian asked Marc "Did you notice that other than the patient, there wasn't a single male at the house? What's up with that?"

"Yep. It's a bizarre sub-culture. Male figures are never around. There were three pregnant women in that house. No baby-daddy anywhere to be seen. I don't know where they are, but I do notice all the men that sit on milk crates on the neutral ground drinking beer all day. I guess that's where they are. I don't understand how a guy can father a child and have nothing to do with it, or sit and do nothing all day, but I quit wondering about it because you and I will never find an answer."

"I just don't get it," Brian said in wonderment.

"Neither do I. But, welcome to New Orleans. Did you ever realize how deeply *laizzez-faire* went?" Marc replied, referring to the old New Orleans attitude that described the general apathy towards just about everything not involving food or music, translated "let things be."

Brian thought for a second and said "I grew up my whole life here, but I had no idea what people were really like. Prayer is one thing, but that kind of ignorance and stupidity... that takes work to accomplish! You have to really *want* to stay ignorant to be like that family."

"Yes, you do. Get used to it."

Their next patient was a homeless man squatting in an abandoned house. He was lying on a discarded mattress, surrounded by empty styrofoam food boxes and liquor bottles. He smelled powerfully of urine and body odor, but oddly didn't smell of feces. He was quite alert and oriented but appeared to be immobile, as the nearby boxes and bottles indicated. He had gotten another homeless friend to call 911 for "leg swelling."

Marc examined his bare feet, they seemed slightly swollen and red, but reasonably healthy other than the apparent cellulitis. He noticed discolored Ace wraps around his lower legs. "What are your legs bandaged up for?"

He answered "I got those wrapped up when I went to the hospital for cuts on my leg after I got hit by a car. They gave me stitches."

"These bandages look pretty old," Brian commented. "How long ago did you get stitches?"

"In January," he said.

Brian raised his eyebrows. "January? This is September! You've had those bandages on for eight months?" Brian looked at Marc, who was clearly wondering about what they would find under the bandages.

The homeless man explained, "Well, I been putting iodine on

them. You know, to keep 'em from getting infected." He produced a half empty bottle of Betadine from somewhere among the rubbish on the mattress. He also explained that since he couldn't get around, he had his other homeless buddies bring him food from shelters and church handouts, and they would share their cheap liquor with him.

Marc asked "So you've just been pouring that on the bandages? When were you planning on taking them off?"

"I don't know."

"Oh, man." Marc exclaimed, shaking his head. He rolled up the man's jeans and began cutting away the Ace wraps with his trauma shears. Marc and Brian both expected the stench of rotten flesh to overwhelm them, but there was none. As Marc removed the last of the bandages, he looked closely at the discolored gauze dressing covering the wound where the sutures supposedly were. The gauze moved. It writhed on the man's leg, powered by... something... underneath. Marc opted not to remove the dressing.

"Let's just get him on the stretcher," Marc recommended.

They retrieved the stretcher and donned their "space suits," plastic gowns to protect their clothes and skin from whatever unseen entity was under the animated dressing and whatever other infectious processes were going on inside their patient. Back inside the house, Brian grasped the man under the shoulders and Marc held onto his pants legs to lift him up. Apparently the man was wearing the same pants he was wearing in January when he first was injured; as Marc tried to lift the man's legs, he discovered that the trouser legs were already cut up to the hips. The force of Marc trying to lift an entire man but instead pulling at torn fabric caused him to fall back a step. A few objects flew out of the ripped pants toward the ceiling and scattered around the scene.

Brian studied one of the objects as Marc regained his balance. "Maggots," they both said simultaneously.

"Gross," again simultaneously. "Now we know why he doesn't smell like shit; the maggots have been taking care of that," Marc explained.

Wrapping the man in a sheet like a big burrito helped solve their lifting issues and helped prevent any errantly vectored larvae from landing on them. Marc chose not to start an IV or even check his vital signs. Neither medic even wanted to touch the man and his personal ecosystem. Brian just drove to University Hospital, Marc kept the exhaust fan on and the air conditioner on its maximum setting to keep the most ventilation going through the truck so as to lessen the ammonia smell of urine.

At the hospital, Dr. Lovejoy commented on Marc and Brian's streak of patients with lower extremity issues as she examined the man's legs and removed the brown gauze dressings. Exposed to the cool air of the emergency room, the maggots sought warmer climes and began wriggling vigorously. Several specimens a full inch long wriggled out of the wound in the man's leg and dropped onto the stretcher. Brian retched at the sight of it and ran out the door onto the ramp, barely managing to contain the bile rising in his throat. Marc too felt ill at the sight and turned away, choosing instead to write his report at the nurses' station.

Dr. Lovejoy, on the other hand, seemed positively captivated by the experience. She brushed maggots out of the way to study the wound, her face disturbingly close to the pile of worms. "Well, they've been doing a good job! The wound looks really clean, no infection. They probably saved his life."

Brian had managed to compose himself once again and had come back into the ER as the doctor was commenting. He looked quizzically at her and asked "Saved his life?"

"Yes," she responded, "maggots don't eat living tissue, just the dead tissue along with the bacteria. Since they keep the wound clean, it doesn't get infected. That other guy with the diabetic foot you brought in could have used some of these little buggers," the doctor remarked to Brian, still mesmerized by the little white critters.

"Maggots, huh?" he replied, somewhere between amazement and nausea. "Learn something new every day. It's still pretty gross."

Later in the truck, Brian and Marc discussed their revulsion at the last two calls. Brian exclaimed "It's just amazing how much *nothing* people are willing to do for themselves to the point that their limbs are literally rotting off their own bodies! The only reason that guy couldn't get around was because his legs were rotten, and his legs were rotten because he wouldn't get around! And the other guy... his foot was falling off because he and his family wouldn't do anything about it! And that woman who called us to take her one block after she had just walked over two miles... How can people be so willfully ignorant and lazy? How can you exist that way? I'd rather die than live in that... that... *stagnation*!"

"Brian, I don't know. But so many people for so many generations have been handed everything to them that they've lost the capacity for independence and self-reliance. That in itself is more disgusting to me than any number of maggots or putrefying flesh."

"Why do we tolerate this? Even encourage it? These folks are just as much a parasite as the maggots. At least the maggots perform some useful function, like the doctor was saying."

"I know, man. I've been seeing it for years, and it hasn't changed," Marc said. "If anything, it's gotten worse. Those kids sleeping in the bed earlier? I wouldn't be surprised if I had delivered some of them when they were born. Or if we'll deliver one of those three welfare babies on the way in that house."

Both medics contemplated that thought in silence and frustration. Their contemplation was broken when dispatch called them on the radio for another call, "shortness of breath," uptown.

The patient was a thirty-five year old man with renal failure in need of dialysis. He sat silently in the chair, perfectly awake and in no visible distress. Like earlier, a female family member spoke for him. "He just got out the hospital."

"For what? And when?" Marc asked.

"The same thing. He just got out two days ago."

"When was your last dialysis?" Brian asked the patient.

"Tuesday," the woman interjected.

"Where do you go for dialysis?" Brian pursued.

"He ain't got no dialysis place here. That's my cousin; he's been stayin' with us a couple weeks. He moved here from Houston and never got no dialysis doctor here."

"So how have you been getting dialyzed?" Marc pursued, trying to direct the questions to the patient, rather than the "spokeswoman."

She replied again for the man, "He gets his dialysis at the hospital. That's why he was there. He's my cousin and he just moved down here from Houston," repeating herself.

"You didn't plan for a doctor or a dialysis clinic here? You just go to the emergency room three times a week?" Marc inquired, trying to keep his impatience in check, for he knew what the answer would be.

"No, he just asks me to call the ambulance to take him to the hospital."

Marc closed his eyes and exhaled slowly. "What hospital does he go to?"

"He went to Baptist last time, but he said he wants to go to Touro today. He was at University before that."

"Okay," Marc responded, at his patience' end. Any further questions would simply serve to irritate him more. He went with Brian to retrieve the stretcher out of the ambulance.

At the back of the truck, Brian said "Weren't we just now talking about this? Another one who does nothing for himself. And the family can't be bothered either."

"Yup," Marc answered. "More of the same."

Again back in the house, Brian asked the man to sit on the stretcher. The patient sat in the wheelchair, drooping like wilted lettuce. Marc was at the end of his rope and said in a commanding voice, "Dude, I just need you to stand up for one second and plop yourself onto my stretcher. I'm not asking you to do any gymnastics."

The man lifted up his head, groaning, trying to give the impression that this simple movement was the heaviest burden since Atlas bore the world on his shoulders. Marc had had enough. Even Brian appeared exasperated, rolling his eyes and shaking his head. "Just pick him up and get this over with," Marc ordered, grasping the man under the arms as Brian grabbed under his knees and planted him onto the stretcher.

In the back of the truck, Brian checked his vital signs and applied the EKG electrodes. The man's EKG was a little slow and the complexes appeared wider than they should be, a typical sign of hyperkalemia, which is common in dialysis patients. Simply eating a banana has been known to send dialysis patients over the edge into a cardiac emergency with its extra potassium. In maneuvering himself in the seat in the ambulance, Marc's clipboard slipped off his lap. As he picked it up and replaced it, his hand knocked against the purloined vial of potassium in his pocket, the one he had lifted from the hospital some days earlier.

He stopped writing for a moment, staring at the clipboard, lost in thought. With an unemotional expression, he looked closely at the patient, then at Brian. "Go ahead and start an IV."

Chapter 6

Terrell looked around the back of the ambulance, wondering when they were going to get on the road. He had grown accustomed to the EMS routine: vital signs, the lengthy series of questions, the EKG monitor, the occasional IV or oxygen. He had grown weary of answering all the questions by his third ambulance ride to get his dialysis, so he just let his cousin speak for him. *I just want a ride to get my dialysis; why do they need to ask all those questions every time?* He heard the paramedic's voice behind him ask the other one to start an IV. *'Man, that shit hurts!'* Terrell thought. He felt the cool of the alcohol, the bite of the needle. He laid on the stretcher, almost motionless.

"I'm ready to go when you are," Marc told Brian.

"Okay. We're going to Touro, right?" he asked.

"Yes," Marc answered. He considered the route there. They were in the Riverbend neighborhood, in the little triangle near Carrollton and St. Charles. "Probably easiest to just head up Leake to Magazine. That's smoother than taking St. Charles all the way." Marc knew that that route was indeed smoother, but would take much longer than driving up St. Charles, with Magazine Street's constant congestion, especially at this time of day, when all the kids were getting out of school, and a little extra time was what Marc needed.

Brian hopped in the driver's seat and started heading to the hospital. Marc watched out the tiny window into the cab until he was sure that Brian was committed to Magazine Street after heading up the river road. He was pleased that the traffic jam started at Audubon Park. The few drivers that weren't oblivious to the ambulance with blazing lights and blaring sirens behind them tried to pull out of the way, but there was nowhere for them to pull over since cars were parked all down the side of the road. The ambulance inched along, ridiculously slowly.

'Perfect,' Marc thought. '*This asshole came to my city to live off us like a parasite. Can't be bothered to have a job, or prepare for his dialysis, or do anything productive. And he's gonna act like he's dying, but he's well enough to get here from Houston and get his Medicaid and Louisiana Purchase card after being here for only two weeks. And his family can't be bothered with him either. This is a problem than needs to be eliminated.*'

Terrell looked out the back window of the ambulance from the stretcher. The paramedic was doing something; he didn't know or care what. Some kind of medication he was injecting into the IV line. The ambulance crews that had picked him up before sometimes did that, gave him medicine in his IV or sprayed that stuff under his tongue. '*Letting them do all that saves me the trouble of taking all those pills they prescribe,*' he thought. A second later, though, a searing pain burned up his arm where the IV was. "Goddamn!" He screamed. "What..." he began to ask, but his voice trailed off as an incredibly heavy burning agony set in his chest. He felt like he was suffocating; it took all his energy to draw in a few deep breaths. His vision began to cloud as he tried to make eye contact with the paramedic. The paramedic was looking over at the screen of the EKG monitor, which was making all kinds of noise that melded with the screech of the siren. '*What's happening?*' he thought to himself. A moment later, despite the pain and the confusion, he could no longer maintain conscious thought and lapsed into the deepest sleep of all.

Marc looked at the monitor. The electrical waves indicating the patient's heartbeat widened and slowed as the patient thrashed on the stretcher. He reached over and turned down the volume on the heart rate alarm. He grasped the patient's wrist and felt for a pulse. He felt two beats, spaced about ten seconds apart, then nothing. The patient stopped thrashing and laid on the stretcher, his dead eyes open and staring in Marc's direction. Marc put his face low to the patient's ear and whispered "The world will be a better place without you." He then put his head in the little window into the cab and told Brian "I guess he was sicker than we thought; he just coded."

Brian glanced into the rearview mirror, eyebrows raised. "What?! I was wondering what all that commotion was. How could he have coded?"

"I don't know, man. I got it though; just keep driving. Let dispatch know."

Marc set about his routine of working a fake code in the back of the truck. He intubated the patient but didn't hook up the Ambu bag to ventilate the patient. He gave a few chest compressions to crack a couple of ribs. He placed the carbon dioxide monitor in his mouth and breathed through it and printed a strip to indicate the chest compressions and normal gas exchange for his report. Since the patient was asystolic, flatlined, Epinephrine and Atropine were indicated as the first drugs to use. He injected them into the wheel well, where they dribbled out the drain onto Magazine Street. Since the patient was on dialysis, he pushed a syringe of calcium chloride into the drain too, since dialysis patients were chronically low on serum calcium. He was regarded as an excellent paramedic for thinking of little things like the calcium; many paramedics just stuck to the minimum required drug algorithms, without considering the correctable causes of asystole. *'Of course, the other paramedics actually inject the drugs and probably don't cause cardiac arrest by giving a potassium bolus,'* he chuckled to himself as he squirted another Atropine into the wheel well. He called Touro to describe his patient so they could prepare for the incoming cardiac arrest.

As they turned the corner onto Prytania Street a block from the hospital, Marc hooked up the Ambu bag and attached the carbon dioxide monitor after giving a few breaths to blow off the excess CO2. He printed another strip from the monitor, which still showed a flat line. *'Naturally it's asystole, he's had no blood flow for fifteen minutes!'* thought Marc, satisfied with his handiwork.

Marc's run report, as usual, merely said the patient's EKG rhythm changed from sinus bradycardia to asystole. He documented the intubation as successful, which it was, but left out the part about not ventilating the patient with oxygen. He recorded the drugs he had shot into the drain as being given exactly on time, with no mention of the one drug he had actually given, potassium chloride. He stapled his EKG strips to the page, which proved he had given chest compressions and had a good intubation. It had gone perfectly. After half a day of dealing with idiots, he was in a much better mood for the rest of his shift. *'The world is already a better place,'* he pondered.

After they had cleared, dispatch told them to remain at Touro to cover the uptown area. Marc smoked a cigarette and chatted with Grace and Cindy, who had also dropped off a patient at Touro. Brian told of his last patient, how he seemed perfectly fine but died anyway. Cindy remarked "Yeah, it's weird how that sometimes happens. I had this lady last week who complained of leg pain after surgery. I thought she just wasn't taking her pain meds; you know the type who 'don't believe in medications?' Well, turns out she had a big ol' blood clot in her vein and chose that moment to throw a P.E. The clot traveled to her lungs and she coded five minutes after putting her on the stretcher. We worked her and all, but she was DRT- Dead Right There," Cindy elaborated. "Nothing you can do. When it's time, it's time."

"Dude, why did that guy code?" he asked Marc, still bewildered by their patient's sudden death.

Marc came up with a story that sounded plausible. "Well first of all, he was on dialysis. Dialysis patients live with one foot in the grave anyway, with no way to eliminate all the toxins that build up. Second, he was non-compliant with his meds. He couldn't be bothered getting his prescriptions filled or getting a regular dialysis clinic. Third, I doubt he was compliant with the special diet you need when you're on dialysis and probably smoked crack on top of that, so I'm sure he was hyperkalemic, too much potassium. His EKG indicated that," Marc explained, and thought to himself *'I'm definitely sure about the potassium.'*

"It's just weird that we've had two patients code on us in a week," Brian said.

"That's right, y'all coded Sparrowhawk last week, huh?" Grace chimed in. "You're on a winning streak! Two dirtbags in one week!" She exclaimed enthusiastically. "I'd like to code Michael Sexton. I picked his nasty ass up every shift last week."

"That guy is so gross!" Cindy said, remembering the daily runs to Canal and Royal Street, the same hangout as Aaron Sparrowhawk and a half dozen other regulars haunted. "Michael Sexton, Deborah Gill, Warren April, Johannes Sunville, David Spencer, all those frequent fliers from down there."

"Not David! David died a couple months ago! I coded him," Marc replied brightly.

"Wow, you get to kill all the roaches!" said Grace.

Marc and Brian chuckled at Grace's reference to the homeless, jobless, drunken bums as roaches. It was said that roaches would be one of the only living things that would survive a nuclear war. EMT's shared a common vision of that post-apocalyptic world, with their frequent-flier patients wandering about, perfectly fine after the deadly nuclear explosions, along with the cockroaches scurrying along the ground.

Grace and Cindy cleared from their call and left Brian and Marc to their own devices. Brian was hungry and headed to Juan's for a burrito. Marc followed him into the restaurant to get a drink. Brian placed his order and Marc said "We're gonna get a call now."

Exactly two seconds after Marc had said that, dispatch called them over the radio. "Stand by to copy," Hope, the dispatcher, said through the radio static.

"Dude, what the hell?" asked Brian, frustrated. "I'm starving!"

"You ordered food. Trying to get food or sitting on the toilet is the equivalent of doing a rain dance. You're begging the EMS gods for a call. Only the EMS gods are way happier to give you a call than the weather gods are to grant you rain. I'm surprised you haven't learned that by now," Marc replied, drawing on his many years of experience with that very phenomenon.

Brian cancelled his order and they both left to respond to the call, a motor vehicle accident. Brian cursed at the other drivers on the road. As they approached a red light, a blue Nissan Armada that had been stopped for it ahead of them began to back up towards the ambulance. "What the hell!" shouted Brian. "Backing up? Towards the ambulance?" Eventually the driver determined that backing up at the intersection was not the way to go, and crept forward. All the other traffic was stopped for the ambulance, drivers on the cross street waved at the Nissan in the way of the unit, motioning for him to go through. It inched ahead and pulled to the left instead of the right, and stopped again, blocking the cross street, which was exactly where Brian needed to turn.

"GOD DAMN IT!" Brian shouted, sounding the air horn at the idiotic driver. "On the damn cell phone, too! I might have known!"

"My, you *are* hungry," Marc said evenly, laughing at Brian's frustration. "You're not your usual, cheerful self."

"Yes, I really wanted something to eat. Plus I'm still wondering about why that guy died."

The smile left Marc's face. He didn't count on his partner being naïve to help cover up what he did, but he always made sure the circumstances were right and there was a good explanation for the patients' sudden death. *'But was I too hasty with that one?'* he wondered. He replied to Brian, "Don't worry about it; people die every day. Especially chronically sick, non-compliant people like him. Don't let this job get to you. You haven't been in it long enough to get all burnt out like me."

"I guess you're right," Brian answered. "I guess I'm just trying to figure out the clinical aspects of it, you know, the mechanics of it. It's just that he seemed fine and now he's dead. That, and I'm still hungry."

"We'll get you something after this call. I'll be hungry by then too," Marc reassured Brian.

Just then, another call came out on the radio for a different ambulance. Marc and Brian listened to the information. The other call was at the same intersection they had passed a few minutes ago. "St. Charles and Washington, for a blue Nissan that struck a streetcar pole."

Marc howled with laughter. "That's the stupid car that wouldn't get out of our way! He must have hit the pole with all his idiotic maneuvering! You see? Kharma's a bitch! You feel better now?"

Brian laughed too. "I do, actually."

They continued their shift, running the usual calls and surprisingly managed to get food. The motor vehicle accident they had been sent on was uneventful, with two patients that wanted transport so it would "look better" for their personal injury lawsuit. Later they brought an elderly woman feeling dizzy to the hospital, and an elderly man who was nauseated, pronounced a gunshot victim dead on scene, and picked up Michael Sexton from Canal and Royal. It took Brian and Marc about a half an hour to clean the truck after Sexton, since he decided to have drunken diarrhea while on the way to the hospital. Marc remained complacent, though. He had managed to rid the world of Terrell, and despite the busy day and majority of dumb calls, he felt accomplished.

Brian's mood had improved after obtaining food, but he still wondered about Terrell, the dialysis patient who had died on them. After finishing his shift at midnight, he drove home to his apartment. His girlfriend, Tammy, was there, preparing to go to bed. She was a pretty young thing, twenty-four, the same age as Brian, with long curly auburn hair, green eyes, small but perky breasts and shapely legs. Brian was a handsome young man too - blonde hair, blue eyes and a wiry swimmer's physique. One day, they would have beautiful kids together.

"How was your day?" Tammy asked.

"Busy. Lots of bullshit, as usual. Pronounced a guy dead, though. Shot through and through the head, brains everywhere," he said, referring to the gunshot victim he and Marc had pronounced dead. "And I puked because of a patient, too. We had this guy with maggots crawling all over him..."

"Oh my God," cried Tammy. "Was he dead or something?"

"No, he was perfectly alive. Stunk to high heaven.

Apparently the maggots were a good thing, according to the doctor."

"I don't want to hear about it. That's disgusting," Tammy said, holding her hand up in a "stop" gesture.

"Sorry, but you asked. And one guy who died in the unit. I was driving and couldn't do anything, but I can't get it out of my head."

"Oh, no, you're not bringing your work home with you, are you?" Tammy jested.

"No, it's just that for the life of me, I can't figure out why he died."

"Well what happened?" Tammy asked.

"He was this dialysis patient who needed dialysis," Brian responded. "He didn't have a clinic here; he was from out of town. But he had been dialyzed two days before, so he hadn't missed any dialysis or anything. We put him in the ambulance and on the way to the hospital my partner told me he had just coded."

"Well what was wrong with him?" Tammy inquired, now genuinely curious.

"That's the thing, nothing was wrong with him. I checked his vital signs myself and his blood pressure was high but nothing deadly. His heart rate was a tiny bit slow but looked pretty okay on the monitor. And he was completely awake. Didn't talk much and just sat there and made us do everything for him. He was very annoying, but I can't figure out why he died."

"Did you ask your partner about it?" Tammy pursued.

"Yeah, Marc thinks he was a crackhead or something, but crackheads usually have a fast heartbeat. And he wasn't taking any of his meds, but he seemed pretty stable to me, even for someone on dialysis not taking his meds. It's just *weird*!" Brian explained. "I don't know, maybe it'll make more sense when I go through paramedic school."

Tammy sat on the bed and thought to herself while Brian showered and got ready to go to sleep. He climbed into bed and they held each other. Tammy noticed Brian staring at the ceiling, awake. "What's wrong?" she asked.

"I'm still thinking about it. I'm sorry," he sighed.

Tammy thought about Brian's story again. "Do you think your partner did something that might have caused him to die?"

Brian looked at her incredulously. "What? No way! Marc's one of the best paramedics at the service! I've seen him save a lot of lives, even among all the bullshit calls we run. Plus I'm right there the whole time. I'd see if anything was... amiss."

"Sorry," she apologized. "It's just that you said it happened while you were driving, so you weren't actually there. I guess I read too many murder mystery novels."

Brian smiled at her. "No, Marc's been there forever and he's way too good of a paramedic. I'm sure he was right; people just die sometimes. He couldn't do anything like that."

He turned to her and closed his eyes to go to sleep.

'Could he?'

Chapter 7

"Forty year-old male with a gunshot wound to the left upper arm and left forearm. He's awake and alert, blood pressure ninety over forty-two, heart rate's one twelve. The bystanders said it was an AK-47; I believe 'em. It's a huge wound," Brian announced as they rolled their patient into the doors of Room Four, the trauma resuscitation room at University.

"Anything else you wanna tell them?" Marc asked quietly.

Brian pondered for a second. "He's got two IV's; saline and Ringer's, sixteen gauges, both on the right. No history or meds, he's allergic to sulfa drugs," he completed as they moved the victim onto the hospital stretcher. "Oh, and merry Christmas, by the way."

"Pretty good," Marc complimented Brian on his report. "Is that your first Room Four report?"

"My first real one. The other ones weren't really injured too bad," Brian answered. "They were Room-Foured just because of the mechanism of injury."

"Looks like you're actually learning something in paramedic school. That's a refreshing change. My course was more like a self-study program. What are you studying now?"

"Acid-base balance. It sucks."

Marc groaned sympathetically. "Oh man, that part really sucks. Once you understand it, it's not too bad, but learning it is awful."

"So am I ever going to need to know that acid-base stuff to work as a paramedic?" Brian inquired.

"Nope. You'll never need it again," Marc answered.

"Then why are they making us learn it?" Brian asked, irritated.

"Probably because your instructors were forced to learn it too, and they want to pass the joy on to you."

"Well, it sucks," Brian continued as he cleaned the stretcher. "I eat, sleep and breathe EMS between work and paramedic class for the last three months and I'm getting sick of it."

Marc grinned as he continued writing his report. "Being a paramedic doesn't get you burned out; paramedic school does. You're preaching to the choir, buddy. Been there, done that."

As Marc got the nurse to sign his report; dispatch was already calling for them on the radio to clear for another call. Brian gritted his teeth as he listened to the information, a "man down" in the Central Business District. "Can't I even get the stretcher back in the truck before you give me another call?" he growled to himself as he tried to hastily get the rest of the truck back together.

When they got to the scene, they found one of their regulars, Johannes Sunville. He was passed out on the sidewalk with his empty bottles of booze strewn around him. His pants used to be blue jeans, but were now stained brown with tobacco stains from cigars he would pick out of the trash and gutters and keep in his pocket, and from feces that had cascaded from his butt all the way down to his ankles. Brian and Marc knew they were the same pants he had been wearing for the last two weeks, since this was the ninth time in fourteen days they had been called for Johannes. Each time they had picked him up, the brown stains were a little larger. Now they covered the entire garment. Johannes was given unclaimed clean clothes from the hospital every so often, since he never bathed or even used a proper toilet. He wasn't retarded or handicapped or psychotic; he was just a drunk who insisted on living his life that way, despite all the help that was offered and available.

Johannes stirred as Marc rolled him over onto his back. "So we meet again," Marc said as Johannes tried to speak, but only slurred some vowels. Marc dodged Johannes' breath, which smelled like he had been dining at the shit buffet. The proximity of the rest of Johannes' body offered little respite from the smell, as encrusted as he was with old wet tobacco and excrement in varying stages of freshness. As the two medics briefly assessed for injuries, it occurred to them how long it would take to air out the ambulance after this transport. "I'm going to obviate this problem right now," he asserted to Brian. Marc pulled out his trauma shears and began cutting every stitch of clothes off Johannes. Brian followed suit and began cutting too, until Johannes was lying bare-naked on Magazine and Poydras Streets. They lifted him onto the stretcher and covered him with a sheet, partly out of respect for the bystanders who might be offended by the naked man before them, but mostly to contain the remaining aroma within the little cocoon the sheet formed.

The chilly December air roused Johannes a bit as they loaded him into the ambulance. He managed to lift up his head and slurred his usual protest: "I jus' wanna die!"

Marc responded without even looking up, "That's okay, Johannes, we want that too," as he copied Johannes' information onto his run report.

Johannes continued insisting he wanted to die, as he always did when he was conscious enough to form words. Marc usually thought it ironic that he would make such a request of him, of all people. Johannes clearly deserved it, but for one fact: Johannes was a retired Army major. He had served in Vietnam for several tours of duty. He still received his retirement pay and, not really having much overhead in the form of rent or bills, was able to use his retirement income to purchase really good booze to swill in the gutter. On this particular occasion Brian kicked away an empty bottle of Ketel One vodka that Johannes had downed.

Brian checked Johannes' vital signs while Marc wrote his paperwork. Afterwards, Brian looked Johannes up and down and with a dejected look asked Marc "Why are we keeping him alive? I mean, if he chooses to live this way; why is it *our* problem that he gets falling down drunk every day? This dude's about as useful as the garbage he lays in on the street. I'm in paramedic school to save lives, but *this* is what I do? Take every homeless, wretched drunk to the hospital every day so they can go out and do it all again tomorrow?"

Marc looked back meaningfully at Brian. "I hear ya, man. It's not what I bargained for either. To be honest, I don't know why we try to keep these fragments of humanity alive either, even when they themselves say 'I wanna die.' And the best part is that yours and my tax dollars go to pay for their ride and hospital bill! This guy lives off his military retirement, which you and I provide by paying taxes, and he lives in the gutter and drinks his Ketel One, which I can't even afford."

"This shit is broken, man!" exclaimed Brian.

Marc's face hovered on the verge of a smile as he thought to himself *'Brian's getting hit hard by the reality of EMS. Paramedic school and full-time work is quickly changing his happy, do-good outlook. I kinda like it.'*

Marc looked back down at Johannes who had slipped back into drunken unconsciousness. *"Who am I to decide that his wish to die is wrong? Even Brian realizes this guy has no place among society."* The circumstances weren't right to put Johannes out of everyone's misery at the moment, though. They were only going to Tulane, a three-minute ride from where they were. There wouldn't be enough time to make it seem like Johannes' death was legitimate, and the brief transport time would increase his chances of survival when the staff began to work on him in cardiac arrest. Up to now, Marc had considered ending Johannes' failure of an existence, but circumstances were never right for the task. And there was the fact of Johannes' honorable military service. Johannes had contributed to society. *'But at what point is that null and void?'* Marc wondered. *'He's now clearly useless to society, and probably extracting far more from the world than he ever put in. He even says he wants to die. How can his life be judged with such different extremes to consider?'*

Marc's reverie was cut short when the ambulance stopped on the ramp of Tulane Hospital. He had gotten so distracted by his own thoughts that he had forgotten to write the rest of his report. When Brian opened the rear doors of the unit, the cool air roused Johannes once again. As the stretcher came out the back of the ambulance, Johannes took in his surroundings and exclaimed once more, "I just wanna die!" before lapsing back into unconsciousness.

As they waited for a bed in the ER, Marc found himself lost in thought again. It had been three months since Terrell's death. Brian had interrogated Marc about the unusual-seeming death, so Marc had decided not to render his "special therapy" to anyone. Since starting his paramedic class, though, Brian had been too preoccupied with classes and studying to bring up the topic again. After three months of transporting Johannes and Michael and Deborah and so many other societal parasites, Marc wondered when the time would be right again to begin to get rid of the chronic drains on the world.

Marc turned around to see his stretcher empty. "Where the hell is our patient?" he asked Brian, who was cleaning it and replacing the stretcher linen.

"He got a room. I told you but you seemed pretty lost in your own little world there, so I just moved him myself," Brian explained.

"Oh, okay, thanks. Sorry. I guess I was a little caught up," Marc apologized.

A few minutes later another call came out for them. An attempted suicide; "your patient took an unknown amount of Percodans," Hope said over the radio.

"Ten-four, en route from Tulane," was Marc's reply.

"A bunch of Percodan?" Brian asked while driving to the scene. "Why can't people do something that'll really kill them if they want to kill themselves? Like shoot themselves in the head or hang themselves? And there's no shortage of tall buildings and bridges to jump off of around here."

"Oh, don't get me started on that!" Marc answered. "I so want to write a book called 'Suicide: How to Do It Right.' All these dummies who take a handful of painkillers... that's just stupid. Interestingly, one of the most efficient ways to kill yourself on pills is with TCA's - tricyclic antidepressants. The ironic thing is they're prescribed for chronically depressed patients - those most at risk for suicide. They give them the best meds to do it with!"

Brian looked at Marc, interested. "Really? Have you seen a lot of those?"

"No," he answered, "a few, but most of those patients have the good drugs to kill themselves with, but instead take a bottle of penicillin or vitamins or something. No wonder they're depressed; they can't even figure out the one thing we all have to do - die. I would add 'pay taxes,' but most of our patients have never had a job, so they never pay taxes."

Brian chortled at Marc's observations as they pulled up to the scene. Their patient was a nineteen year-old kid standing at the police car that was already on scene. An officer met Marc at the truck and said he had taken twenty-eight Percodans. When speaking to the patient, the kid told Marc it was more like ten. Either way, he had the telltale chalky white coating on his lips that said he had tried to overdose on something.

"Okay, if the police take the handcuffs off, are you going to behave?" Marc asked the boy.

"Yes, sir" he responded.

The boy climbed into the ambulance and was quite calm and cooperative. As Marc interviewed him, he realized that the boy was pretty nice, with a concerned family. His mother had called 911 after discovering his plans to try to off himself with his Percodans, which he was taking for an injured knee. The police had handcuffed him to protect him from hurting himself further. The boy had been depressed; apparently he couldn't find a job and was suffering the same malaise that Marc often felt when he had been off work for more than a few days. "Well, I can certainly understand how you feel," he informed him. "If I'm off work for a while, I get pretty depressed too."

A few quiet minutes ticked by on the way to the hospital. Halfway there, the boy spoke up and inquired of Marc, "Sir, if I asked you to kill me, would you do it?"

Marc looked at him, stunned. In the moment before answering the boy, a hundred thoughts raced through his mind.

'Would I kill him? How many have I already? Those deserved it; they were the dregs of society who never contributed a thing to the world. How bizarre that this kid would ask ME, of all people, to kill him. But he's just a kid, he has a decent family and he's depressed because he DOESN'T have a job. That's not a reason to get rid of him; if anything, I admire his desire to be a productive human being.'

Marc composed his response. "You don't really want to die. You're just feeling what every other kid feels at some point growing up. I know I felt the same way sometimes when I was your age. But trying to off yourself isn't the answer. Besides, a handful of painkillers isn't going to really hurt you..."

"Well can you give me some pointers on how to do it?" he asked.

Marc laughed out loud. "I don't think that it would be very ethical of me to tell you how to do it right, so no. But you told me you're depressed because you don't have a job. The solution to that isn't trying to die; the solution is tackling the problem - find yourself a job. I think it's great that you care that strongly about it. Instead of trying to avoid your problems like this, face them and overcome them. Your family is obviously willing to help you, too. Use all that to your advantage and you'll be great."

The young man thought about Marc's words for a minute, and brightened visibly. "I guess you're right," he said, smiling. "Thank you, sir."

Marc laughed again and the patient laughed a little with him, sheepishly realizing what a childish thing he had done. He wanted to be a man, but just had a hard time realizing how to act like one. He would be fine. Marc felt good too, and smiled as he gave his report to Mignon, the triage nurse. He hadn't "done" anything, no IV's, no medications, no oxygen, not even an EKG, but he knew he had made a difference in someone's life for the better, and those were the moments he loved his job.

It was a Sunday, and Marc knew that sooner or later he and Brian would be responding to a church. Four calls had already come out throughout the day for other units to respond to churches and their panoply of congregational issues - seizures, pass-outs, weakness... whatever "gift" the Holy Spirit saw fit to bestow upon the faithful. Marc and Brian were sent to the New Zion Greater Light of Jesus First Baptist Missionary Church for a female that had passed out.

On the way, Brian commented "I wonder where the 'Old Zion Lesser Light of Jesus First Baptist Missionary Church' is?"

Marc grinned. "Maybe the Greater Light church pays their light bill on time."

They both laughed; Brian observed "Do all these little ghetto churches try and outdo each other with their names? I mean really, that's a lot of signage, if you ask me."

"Hah!" Marc chuckled. "There used to be one out in the east called "Smoking for Jesus Ministries.' How do you like that one?"

"Really? What were they smoking?"

"Mmm," Marc responded, putting up his hands in an 'I'm not even going there' gesture.

At the church, the fire department had responded also. Marc, Brian, four firefighters, the ambulance stretcher, and various equipment crowded the center aisle of the little church as the preacher went on in his sermon and all the black church ladies in their very impressive hats hollered "Amen!" and "Praise Jesus!" and whatever other incantations were acceptable in the New Zion Greater Light of Jesus First Baptist Missionary Church.

Marc and Brian and the firemen tried to focus on their task of getting the patient secured to a spineboard, since she had hit her head on the pew when she passed out and could conceivably have a spinal injury. It felt like it was taking forever to Marc; there were too many people and too much equipment in the way. He was on the outskirts of the group of first responders, too far from the patient to do anything useful. He was closest to the pulpit with his back turned to the preacher, watching Brian and the firemen attach the cervical collar and spineboard. He half-listened to the preacher's words behind him, not having much else to do.

"MENE, MENE, TEKEL, PARSIN. This is the interpretation of the thing: MENE; God hath numbered thy kingdom, and finished it. TEKEL; Thou art weighed in the balances, and art found wanting..." were the words of the preacher, reading from the book of Daniel.

Brian, to Marc's left and nearer the patient along with two of the firemen, turned their faces toward Marc and stared at him for a second. Marc had spoken the same words as the preacher, out loud, apparently without even thinking about it. Marc composed himself and turned back to the task at hand. "Sorry, got distracted," he whispered.

"What, are you the deacon now or something?" Brian joked quietly, a quizzical look on his face.

As they finally got the patient secured to the board and moved onto the stretcher, all six heard the preacher boom over the speakers "Ain't no way it takes an ambulance a half an hour to pick up one person. Disruptin' the Lord's service..."

As they rolled out the door, Brian spoke without looking back "Is the preacher bitching at us from the pulpit?"

Marc nodded. One of the firefighters answered "It sure sounds that way to me. Wow." Brian turned to the preacher from the door and when he made sure he had made eye contact with the minister, he mouthed "You're welcome" to the preacher.

In the back of the truck, Marc and Brian both commented on the preacher complaining about them to his entire congregation while they worked to help a member of that congregation. "Was he mad at us because we were taking her away before the collection plate had been passed?" Marc said.

"I can't believe that he was saying that while we were trying to help his own people! Saying we're 'disruptin' him for a half hour; we were only on scene for ten minutes!" Brian noted.

"Yeah, that's our community's spiritual leaders for ya. Great example for the church. And people wonder why New Orleans is so corrupt and crime-ridden." Marc added.

Back at the hospital, Marc excused himself to the bathroom

and asked Brian to start getting the patient triaged. Brian told Mignon about the preacher complaining about them in front of the whole church. "The whole church?" she asked. "Is it because y'all were white?"

"No, all the firemen were black and he was bitching at them too. Said we took a half-hour when we were only there for ten minutes." Brian sighed and quit talking about it. "Whatever. I'm over it."

Mignon, a friendly, bubbly, blond girl, put on an exaggerated look of sympathy. "Aww, poor baby! Is paramedic school getting to you? Do you hate everyone now?"

Brian smiled at the joke. "How long have you known Marc?" he asked her.

"A while. Since he started doing EMS, almost twenty years ago. Why?" she asked, more serious.

"Has he ever been given to bouts of... religious fervor?" Brian asked, not sure how else to phrase it.

"Marc? Not that I know of. Why, was he overcome with the Holy Spirit too, like your patient?" joking again.

"No, it was just kind of weird. I noticed him speaking the same words as the preacher as he read out of the Bible. Never took Marc for a holy kinda guy. He knew the words by heart."

Mignon thought for a minute. "Lots of people can quote something from the Bible. That's not strange."

"Yeah, I guess not. Just... unexpected," Brian responded.

In the restroom, Marc washed his hands and face, checking himself in the mirror. The preacher's words reverberated in his head. *'You have been weighed in the balance, and have been found wanting.'* It had been so long since he had read those words, yet he could still quote them.

'I had almost forgotten.'

He thought of his quandary earlier about Johannes. He had been conflicted about Johannes' life. At what point were his years of public service and contributions to the world considered outweighed by his years of selfish consumption? At what point is anyone's?

Marc had used those words as a guide to direct him in who was deserving of having their selfishness ended. He did not consider himself a religious person, nor did he think he was "doing the Lord's work." The words from the book of Daniel simply expressed Marc's feelings exactly, and he had memorized them years earlier in much the same way one learns the lyrics to a song that is particularly resonant and touching. *'God deals with kings. I have to deal with everyone else,'* he reminded himself.

Their shift wore on. Day gave way to night, and the calls continued without a break. Around ten p.m., they were sent to a call downtown for a man struck by a car. The patient was lying in the road, moaning. As the medics approached him, a familiar smell met their noses.

"Johannes!" they said in unison.

"We just brought you to the hospital today!" Brian exclaimed.

"Dish...charred..." Johannes slurred.

"You were discharged? And what? Left to get drunk again? And stumble out into traffic?" Brian shouted, kicking the shattered bottle of Gentleman Jack whiskey on the ground next to Johannes. "Christ, twice in one day!" he commented to Marc.

Marc smiled sympathetically at Brian and asked him to get a spineboard and c-collar. A passing car had sideswiped Johannes as he had drunkenly stumbled into the street. He had an abrasion to his head, chest and right leg where the car had knocked him down. Brian returned with the equipment and they got him secured to it and loaded him in the ambulance.

Marc started an IV while Brian checked his vital signs. "Okay, Johannes, what hospital do you want to go to this time?" Brian asked the nearly unconscious man on the stretcher. He didn't answer. Brian rubbed his knuckles against Johannes' sternum to rouse him. "Where do you want to go?" he shouted.

'Paramedic school IS getting to him,' Marc thought.

Johannes opened his eyes and slurred something. "Ergh...ell...shlih...tell..."

"Slidell?" Brian shouted at Johannes. You want to go to Slidell?"

Johannes looked up at Brian. In his haze, he realized he was being asked a question. He had learned a long time ago that when someone offered you something, you accepted it and said 'yes,' regardless of what they were offering. It was how he had managed to get most of the things he had gotten since retiring - money, food, booze, clothes, whatever. Johannes tried to move his head in the collar and tape in what could be interpreted as a nod.

Slidell was the next town east of New Orleans, in St. Tammany Parish. New Orleans EMS' transport protocols allowed the ambulances to transport out of the parish to the adjoining parishes if the patient requested it. Slidell was about a forty-five minute drive out, and another forty-five minutes back.

"Okay, Slidell it is!" Brian said. *That'll be a nice long drive to finish out our shift. Plus we might be rid of Johannes for a while, till he finds a way back to New Orleans,'* he thought.

Marc nodded to Brian. "Sounds good to me!" he said enthusiastically.

At the hospital, Mignon chatted with Dr. Hunter, a tall, well-built, shaved-headed fellow. They had both been flirting with each other for a while but nothing had ever happened between them. "What time are you finished your shift tonight?" he asked her.

"At eleven. How about you? Interested in getting a drink afterwards?" she answered.

"I'm on till midnight..." He was cut off by the medical control radio he carried on his hip. He was the EMS medical control doctor tonight, and carried the radio to communicate with the ambulance crews in the field. "EMS to med control..." the radio crackled.

"Go ahead. Dr. Hunter here."

"Hey doc, Marc here. We were transporting one of our regulars to Slidell. Sixty year-old male, just got discharged from your hospital today for alcohol intoxication. You know him."

Mignon rolled her eyes. "That's Johannes Sunville! He just got discharged two hours ago! They picked him up *again*?"

Dr. Hunter shook his head, already disgusted. "Go ahead. I copy," he spoke into the radio.

"He got drunk again, walked out into traffic and got sideswiped by a car. Minor abrasions to his head, chest and leg. Initial GCS of 14, blood pressure was one ninety over one-ten, heart rate of one hundred, respirations twenty. Blood glucose ninety-nine. He had requested transport to Slidell but halfway there he coded, went into v-fib. I gave him three shocks; he's in asystole now. He's intubated, got my first line of drugs down. We've turned around and are headed back to you. Should be there in about fifteen minutes. I guess his injuries weren't so minor."

"Okay, we'll see you then," Dr. Hunter answered.

"Holy crap, so Johannes coded? I never thought he'd die!" Mignon said.

Fifteen minutes later, Brian and Marc rolled into Room Four, Brian codesurfing and Marc calling out his report of what drugs had been given and how many defibrillation attempts had been done. Mignon attached the hospital's EKG monitor. It showed a flat line, asystole.

Marc glanced at the monitor. "He's been asystolic since after the first three defibrillations.

"How long have you been working him?" asked Dr. Hunter.

Marc asked dispatch over his radio when he had first advised that his patient was in cardiac arrest. "Twenty-two forty," Hope answered.

Dr. Hunter looked at the clock on the wall. "Twenty minutes. Let's go ahead and call it," he announced to the staff.

Mignon announced for the other nurse who was documenting the event "Time of death, twenty-three hundred."

Brian was cleaning the stretcher and watching the staff. Marc passed him on his way out the door, saying "I'm gonna go clean the truck up."

Marc exited the door, one hand in his pocket, Brian noticed. He still had a perplexed look on his face, since Marc had let him know their patient had coded and they had turned around out in New Orleans East to head back to University, their closest hospital, even though it had been a good fifteen or twenty minutes away.

He felt unsettled. *'Something's wrong,'* a tiny voice said in the deep nether regions of Brian's head. He was tired; they had had a busy shift. He had managed to get nothing to eat, each time he and Marc had attempted getting food, another call came out, causing them to have to cancel three orders at different places. They hadn't even been able to get any coffee. His clothes stunk, as Marc had begun lighting up cigarettes in the ambulance on the way to calls to quell hunger pangs, or because of stress, or both. And Brian had class at eight in the morning. It was no wonder his mind was telling him something was wrong; there was a lot wrong with the entire day's shift. He just wanted to go home and get in bed with Tammy.

He processed all this information and tried to shut up the annoyance in his head. Even so, he could still hear the tiny whisper, *'Something's wrong.'*

Chapter 8

Brian went home and fell asleep quickly. He was too tired to pay much attention to the little voice in his head. It had been an exhausting shift and he had to be up early. No doubt the weirdness was because of being tired. *'Who cares if fucking Johannes Sunville died, anyway? Good riddance.'*

The next morning he went to paramedic class; fortunately it was over by noon. He had signed up to work overtime on Monday and his shift started at 6 p.m., allowing him a nap before work. It would be rough working a full night shift, but he needed the extra money. His partner for the evening would be Joyce, another experienced paramedic who had been at the service as long as Marc had. Joyce was a little older than Marc; she was a formidable-looking black woman, the type whom you would not want to be mad at you. Her accent was a combination of country and ghetto and it reminded Brian of Hattie McDaniels' Mammy character in "Gone With the Wind." Brian had only worked with Joyce a few times, but always enjoyed her as a partner. She carried herself with regal grace, a true southern belle. Anyone who met her knew she would be the *grande dame* of her family.

"Hey baby, how you been?" Joyce greeted him as she put her gear in the truck.

"Tired, Jo. They kicked our ass last night and I had paramedic class today. Hope it's slow," he answered.

"Child, you know bettah than to say da 's' word if you hopin' for a good night. How's yo' momma an' dem? It was sho' nice meetin' her at the crawfish berl."

"Oh she's fine. Tammy said to tell you hi too," Brian mentioned.

"Tell her hi back. Y'all engaged yet? You two'll have some beautiful chirren, you know?"

Brian blushed a little at the compliment. "Thanks, Jo. You ready to go?"

"Whenever you are, baby," she said as she positioned her considerable frame in the passenger seat.

Their first call of the night was for a "baby not breathing." Hope said that they were trying to give CPR instructions over the phone. The address was in the fifth district, on Desire Street, in the middle of the ghetto. They pulled up to the shotgun house; several people were on the front porch drinking, a few others ran out to the ambulance to meet the crew, crying and screaming, pointing into the house.

"This doesn't look good," Brian mumbled to Joyce as he took in the scene.

Joyce walked into the house as Brian collected the gear from the back of the truck. When he arrived in the back bedroom where the patient was, Joyce was already on the medical control radio asking for Do Not Resuscitate orders from the doctor. She informed the doctor that the three month-old baby was asystolic on the EKG monitor even before Brian had attached the leads. As he did so, he noticed that the infant was gray and stiff with rigor mortis. It was a foregone conclusion that the monitor would show asystole; Joyce didn't need to look at an EKG to determine that.

The baby's fifteen year-old mother cried kneeling next to the bed. After Joyce had obtained a time of death from the physician on the radio, she knelt next to the girl and put her arm around her. "Baby, I know this is hard. I been there too; I lost a three month-old baby myself, almost just like this. Died of SIDS. I never thought I'd get over it, just like you feel now."

The teenager looked up at Joyce. Brian could see the empathy registering in her eyes.

"You know, I cried for days when that happened," Joyce continued. "But then I realized that the Lord was tellin' me something. I was only seventeen when I had that baby; the Lord was tellin' me I was too young to be bringin' another life into this world. I couldn't take care of no child. It wasn't fair to that baby. I think He may be telling you the same thing; givin' you a second chance to raise a baby right, when the time's right."

The girl sniffled a bit, still crying, but knelt higher and threw her arms around Joyce. Brian noticed her eyes - they had expressed nothing but inconsolable sadness. Now he saw a tiny glimmer of hope in them. The girl let go of Joyce just as the police were arriving to make their report of the death. Brian and Joyce left, telling the rest of the family they were sorry for their loss as they hauled the equipment back to the truck.

As they drove off, Joyce wrote her report. Brian reviewed the entire scene in his head, and said "I didn't know you had lost a baby. That must have been really hard."

Joyce looked up at him. "I never lost no baby."

Brian raised his eyebrows. "But you told that girl..."

"Well, of course I did. Best way to get her to listen to me is by making her think I had gone through the same thing. She *is* too young to be having babies. All fifteen year-olds are. And the last thing the world needs is another welfare baby. I didn't lie about one thing - a fifteen year-old raising a baby in the ghetto on welfare isn't fair to the baby. I seen it too many times, growing up as a child and every day at work. And calming people down on that scene was important; dat coulda got outta hand real quick. Besides, it don't hurt nothin' to try to make her feel better."

"Where did you grow up?" Brian inquired.

"I'm was raised outside of Lafayette on a farm. When I was ten, my family moved here to New Orleans. We lived in the St. Thomas projects."

"I've heard of the St. Thomas. Marc mentions them all the time. Sounds like it was pretty bad," Brian commented.

"Bad? Baby, you don't know bad. People killed out in the courtyard by my house almost every damn day. All of 'em on drugs. And if dey ain't on drugs, dey was drunk. Me and two other girls from that neighborhood were the only ones not pregnant before we were even eighteen; every other girl got pregnant at thirteen, fourteen; raisin' those po' kids in the projects on welfare, till the kids got old enough to get shot or get pregnant themselves... Tearin' down the St. Thomas was the best thing they coulda done."

Their next call was for a man "passed out," in the lower ninth ward. On scene were several family members on the verge of hysteria. They directed Joyce and Brian upstairs to a man lying face down on the floor. He was drenched in sweat, and barely moaned when Joyce pressed her pen against his fingernail. "He really is out," she said quietly to Brian. "He's diabetic; his blood sugar's low. Let's wake him up here, 'cause I don't wanna carry his heavy ass down them steps."

The family was hovering over Brian and Joyce while they tried to work on the man, so Joyce asked them to fetch his medicine and identification, mostly to get them out of the way. Moments later though, they had returned with fistfuls of medicine bottles, discharge paperwork from previous hospital visits, phone bills, a postcard from Indiana and an assortment of mostly useless documentation. They hurled the stuff at Brian and Joyce, as if they were riding on a Carnival parade float and the EMT's were trying to catch beads. They continued hovering over the medics, fearfully hollering at the patient to "hold on!" and "just breathe!" and "trust in the Lord!"

"I can't work like this," Joyce muttered to Brian. "I'm gonna get them off our backs. You get him going with an IV and D50."

Brian got to work starting an IV on the patient. Joyce had been listening to the family's worried exclamations. She rose, put her arms around the group and said to all of them "Y'all come on out to the other room. Let me talk to you a minute." They followed her out, reminding Brian of a flock following their shepherd. He remained to work on the patient alone.

"Has he been sick lately? Any problems?" Joyce asked, looking deeply into each of the family members' eyes.

"Well, he's a diabetic. And has high blood," one of the women replied.

"He's been under a lot of stress too. His sister died last

month," a man added.

Joyce paused for a second. "I know it's been hard," she said with what sounded like sincerity in her voice. "Y'all need to be strong for him."

"Oh lawd, is he gonna be all right?"

Joyce picked up on their frequent mentions of "the Lord." "He needs strength beyond what y'all can give." She took the hands of the closest two family members and raised up her face, eyes closed. "Dear Jesus, grant this man the strength beyond what is normal..."

The family followed suit, rising their faces, exclaiming in the same way they would at church, "Amen! Yes, Lord!"

"And grant these good people the wisdom and help to assist him in his hour of need..." Joyce continued.

Brian, in the other room, continued his work of starting an IV on the patient. The man's blood glucose was twenty-three, far too low to sustain consciousness. Once the IV was in place, Brian pulled out the big syringe full of Dextrose and injected it into the IV port. While it did its work, he listened to Joyce praying loudly in the other room, and the family hollering "praise Jesus!" and so on. He was glad he had his back to the doorway. 'This is hilarious!' he thought to himself, biting his tongue so as not to laugh out loud. From the back, it appeared as if Brian was performing some medical procedure on the patient. From the front, Brian had tears in his eyes, trying to stifle his laughter.

Joyce finished her prayer with the family. "... and if it be thy will, O Lord, let us see your might at work! Amen!"

"Amen!" the family responded in unison. They all opened their eyes and entered back into the room. The patient was sitting upright on the floor, awake and alert, looking around at the medics and his family. "What happened?" he asked, bewildered. Joyce's "faith healing" was successful.

"Daddy, you're okay!" one of the women shouted.

"Oh praise Jesus! Thank y'all so much! It's a miracle!" another woman proclaimed.

"Whatever you did, it worked!" Brian exclaimed, getting in on the act.

The patient was perfectly fine after the administration of Dextrose and Holy Spirit. Someone went to the kitchen to fetch him some food, as Joyce had recommended. The man didn't want to go to the hospital; Brian took out the IV and rechecked the man's vital signs as the family continued to gush praise at him and Joyce and Jesus.

Back in the ambulance, Brian looked over at Joyce; she stared at him. After a moment, neither could contain it any longer and both laughed hysterically at each other for a good five minutes.

Later on in the night, a call came out for them for another "pass out." When they got to the scene, family and friends were sitting on the porch, chatting with each other, calm and collected. "We'll get cancelled off this call," Joyce informed Brian as they exited the truck.

"Hey, y'all called us?" Brian called to the people on the porch.

"My grandmother caught a seizure. It happens all the time. She's right there in the front room. She's sleeping now," one of the girls on the porch said, then turned back to her friend and continued her conversation with another girl.

Joyce and Brian walked into the house; apparently everyone was outside. The elderly lady in the chair sat motionless. Joyce glanced at Brian and pinched the old lady's shoulder. "Ma'am?" she said. Brian placed his fingers on her neck to feel for a pulse. Her skin was cool, her lips bluish.

"Sleeping?" Joyce whispered. "She's dead as a doornail!"

Brian attached the EKG to print a strip while Joyce went to go talk to the family on the porch. "How long's she been like this?" Joyce asked.

"Oh, Mama's been sleeping for a while. I guess an hour," a woman responded.

Joyce sat on the porch next to the elderly woman's daughter.

"Honey, I have to tell you, yo' mama's expired."

The daughter looked at her, completely oblivious to Joyce's meaning. "Expired? What you mean, expired? Like a credit card?"

Joyce replied "Like a Visa, yes darlin'. She's passed on."

The woman apparently still needed some clarification. "She's dead, honey," Joyce added.

"AAAAHHHH!" screamed the woman. The daughter laid back on the porch and proceeded convulsing. Out of nowhere, the other girl, the granddaughter, produced an enormous soup ladle and began trying to thrust it into the seizing woman's mouth.

"Why you told her that? You know she catches seizures!" hollered the granddaughter.

Joyce was taken aback. "I just met her five minutes ago! I don't know nuthin' 'bout her seizures. Brian, come help me with this."

Brian had gotten an EKG strip and contacted medical control for DNR orders for the dead grandmother. He had been watching the encounter on the front porch from through the door. For the second time tonight, he felt himself struggling to hold back from literally rolling on the floor with laughter.

Once they had extricated the giant cooking instrument from the seizing woman's face, it was apparent they would have to transport their new patient. In the truck, Brian started an IV and Joyce handed him an ampule of Valium. "Just give it all to her," she instructed. "I don't really want to have her all tachylordia and seizing back here. That's just a headache waitin' to happen."

"Tachylordia?" Brian asked as he drew up the medication into a syringe.

"Marc never taught you that? I'm gonna have to have a talk with that boy. You know what tachycardia is, right? A fast heartbeat."

Brian nodded.

"Tachylordia is when they keep shouting 'Oh Lord, oh Lord,

oh Lord!'" Joyce explained.

Brian guffawed so loudly it woke up their patient, who had been snoring on the stretcher after her seizure. She opened her eyes and recognized Brian and Joyce. Once the earlier events had processed in her mind, she spoke up, screeching "Oh mama! Oh Lord, Oh Lord, Jesus! Lord, help me!"

Brian himself was convulsing with laughter, in disbelief at the verbatim fulfillment of Joyce's prediction. "Give her *all* the Valium," she instructed again. "I'll just say in my report that she needed it all 'cause she kept seizing."

After the hefty dose of medication, the woman dozed on the way to the hospital and had no more seizures or tachylordia fits. Brian chuckled almost continuously as he drove, thinking about the outrageous scenarios he had witnessed. He had learned a lot from Marc, especially clinical procedures, report writing, radio communication and how to recognize safe versus unstable scenes. Joyce was teaching him things he never even realized he might need to know. She had stabilized hysterical family members and given life lessons to the young mother with a dead baby, she had quelled fears and made the EMS crew look like heroes to the diabetic's household. And this last scene, well, that was just hilarity drawn from tragedy. Brian never thought he would hear of a corpse being compared to a credit card. But Jo had managed to do so, and he already knew she had provided some of the best memories of EMS he would ever have.

'And the funny thing is that I don't think I've even seen her perform a single medical procedure today!' he thought to himself. Joyce hadn't even so much as checked a pulse on a patient all night, yet she had managed to teach Brian so much in just one shift.

At the hospital, Joyce waited for a room for their patient and Brian cleaned the truck. He collected the dirty needle from the IV off the floor and put it in the sharps container, noticing that the container was beyond full. Needles and syringes protruded out the top of the opening in the counter that led to the sharps box underneath. He tried to push them down into the box, but it was too full. "When we clear we're gonna need to stop by the station for a minute for a new sharps box," he informed dispatch over the radio.

After Joyce had returned with the stretcher, they headed back to the station. Joyce wrote her report on the dead woman while Brian tended to the equipment. The sharps container was secured on a little ledge accessible through an outside cabinet on the ambulance. He pulled it out, holding it by only two fingers, trying to avoid getting stuck by the dirty sharps protruding from the top. One of the syringes caught on the lip of the cabinet, knocking the box out of his hand. It tumbled to the ground, bouncing; Brian jumped back to avoid the needles. The weight of the box filled with surgical steel, blood and glass caused the protective cap to pop off, scattering its contents on the ground.

"Motherfucker!" Brian shouted.

"You okay, baby?" Joyce hollered from inside the truck.

"Yeah, I just spilled all the sharps on the ground. I got it, though." He put on an extra set of gloves and started carefully collecting the needles, empty medication vials and syringes to put them back in the red box. He noticed one empty vial he didn't recognize. *'Potassium Chloride? How did that get in there?'* he wondered. He had thoroughly dissected the bag of medications in the ambulance on a few occasions to familiarize himself with it, but didn't remember seeing any potassium chloride. *'Did they recently add that to our inventory or something? I must have missed that memo.'*

After leaving the station, dispatch sent them to the West Bank to cover the Algiers neighborhood. Algiers was a strange part of the city. For the most part, 911 calls for EMS there were few, but when they did start rolling in, they didn't stop. Algiers could go all day without a single EMS call, then minutes later, all at once have every ambulance in the city on West Bank calls. Brian looked forward to the down time the West Bank offered; he could study or take a nap.

Unfortunately, dispatch had other plans for him and Joyce. Hope called them over the radio for a female with "abdominal pains." When they arrived at the scene, the patient was a twenty-two year-old girl, eight months pregnant. She had purple, dreadlocked hair and a tie-died skirt on. The house had an air mattress on the floor. Other than the air mattress, there was not a stick of furniture in the house. Her boyfriend hovered about the room, obviously stoned, as were the other two people apparently living in the house with them.

"What's goin' on?" Joyce asked.

The boyfriend spoke up. "She's been crying that her belly hurts. I need to find my keys. Honey, where's your bag? Do you guys know where you're bringing her? Where's my cell phone? I'm hungry..." and he blathered on in his marijuana haze as Joyce and Brian tried to ascertain what was wrong with the patient.

"What's goin' on with you, honey? You in labor? What? I need you to talk to me," Joyce said as the girl rolled around on the mattress, boo-hooing and moaning. She was completely awake, but simply refused to talk to the medics.

Joyce quickly grew impatient with the dramatics. She took a deep breath and summoned her most commanding voice, the exact powerful voice Brian was afraid Joyce might use on him. "Girl, get up off dat floor! Sit up and talk to me or I'm walking out dat door right now!"

The girl sat bolt upright, finally silent. The baby-daddy peeked in from the doorway, briefly brought back to reality from his cloud. The other two wide-eyed roommates took a few steps back from Joyce and went outside onto the sidewalk. Brian was happy that The Voice had not been directed at him.

"Girl, why am I here?" Joyce demanded.

"My stomach hurts," she finally said.

"Well, girl, you got seven pounds of baby in there. What'd you expect?" Joyce retorted.

"I need to go to the hospital."

"Well, awright. Get yo' shoes on an' come on," Joyce instructed.

In the ambulance, Brian checked vital signs while Joyce got the girl's information. It was easy to tell the girl wasn't from

New Orleans. "Where are you from?" he asked.

"California. I've been here six months."

"What do you do here?" he pursued.

"Nothing," She answered.

"You don't have a job here?"

She shook her head 'no.' "I'm on disability."

"For what?" Brian asked her.

"I'm bipolar."

"You can get disability for being diagnosed bipolar?" He thought back to many patients and even some personal friends of his that were bipolar. The ones he knew personally were very functional and held steady jobs. "Then why did you come to New Orleans?" he asked, uncertain of why one might make such a long journey to a different city, while pregnant, to do... nothing.

The girl didn't answer; she made a slight shrug with her shoulders, and changed the topic by resuming her crying. Joyce sighed; Brian left the back of the ambulance to drive to the hospital.

After they had cleared from the hospital, Brian asked Joyce "What was the deal with that girl? Why did she come all the way here from California for nothing?"

"'Cause they kicked her off welfare in California. She came here to get our Medicaid and food stamps and welfare and disability payments," Joyce answered.

"What the hell?" Brian asked, incredulous and angry. "Is this city some kind of Mecca for welfare recipients? Every person I pick up who's from out of town and not a tourist is on welfare! These people come here specifically to *not* work. Gee, thanks guys!" He felt the frustration that he had seen in Marc. Only now Marc wasn't there to foster the feeling. Brian's frustration and anger was purely his own.

"I know, child," Joyce empathized. "My family had welfare when we moved to the St. Thomas. But my daddy *hated* accepting help. He had pride about him; a good kind of pride. He

78

and my momma both worked every day to get us out da projects and pay our own way. I cain't understand why dese folks today *try* to get on welfare and handouts, all they can get. They ain't got no pride. Even the animals work to provide for themselves; that girl and folks like her, they worse than dumb animals."

They were again sent to the West Bank to cover that area. Brian pulled out his paramedic textbooks and started studying. His class was covering pharmacology, so he turned to that section. He had already memorized the information on most of the drugs the section covered, especially the ones that the ambulance carried, so he searched for drugs he was unfamiliar with. He remembered the vial of potassium he had found in the sharps box, so he looked for references to it in his text. It was only barely mentioned in a few sections, cardiac function, electrolytes and some mentions of it under disease processes, but he could find no information on its properties or administration techniques.

"Jo, what's potassium chloride used for?" he asked his partner.

She looked up from her magazine. "They mostly just give it to patients that's low on potassium. You need it for yo' cells to function; mostly in the heart."

"Do we carry it on the unit?"

"Oh, Lawd no! That's gotta be mixed and diluted and given on a pump. That's only given in the hospital and they have to be on a cardiac monitor. Some places don't even let the nurses mix potassium. You give it wrong and you kill the patient real quick. I don't even like pushing the electrolytes we do carry, like calcium. Push it wrong and yo' patient's going to the morgue."

Brian went over this information in his head. "Okay, thanks," he told Joyce. *'Then... what in the world was that stuff doing on the ambulance?'* He thumbed through his textbook, not reading the pages, lost in thought. He considered asking Joyce what she thought about finding a vial of potassium chloride on the truck, but remembered the maxim that Marc and every other EMT had ingrained into him since day one: "What happens in the truck stays in the truck." Joyce had pushed no drugs today; Brian had performed all the patient care. Other crews rarely used their ambulance. Marc was the only one who might know about the potassium. He would have to ask Marc about it.

He continued poring over his textbook, hoping to find the missing chapter on potassium. He didn't.

Chapter 9

Brian and Joyce managed to avoid any more calls for the rest of the shift. The West Bank had entered its quiescent phase. Despite the quiet, the last hour of the shift was always the most anxiety-driven. Waiting there for the end of the shift and to go home, but anticipating the possibility of receiving a late call made it impossible for Brian and Joyce to rest or study. You can't do anything productive while you're waiting for something.

Brian was scheduled to work on Wednesday, but Marc had called out sick. He ended up working an uneventful shift with Bryan, the paramedic whose name caused gossip around the station to be incorrectly attributed to Brian. To clarify which name the other employees were talking about, Brian was referred to as "Straight Brian" and Bryan was called "Gay Bryan." Their patient load consisted of mostly elderly people feeling weak during the day, and drunken tourists at night, along with one of their frequent fliers uptown. The most interesting aspect of their shift was the vaguely entertaining times that ER staff would say "Hey, Bryan," and both medics would answer.

Brian had to call out sick on Friday; he wasn't really sick, but paramedic class had taken a lot out of him and needed to rest. He had class every day he was off, and the night shift with Joyce had wrecked his internal body clock. With Brian out sick, Marc would work with Gay Bryan that day. Gay Bryan worked the other swing shift on a similar schedule as Marc and Straight Brian, ten a.m. to midnight, three days a week.

"Nice to work on a double-paramedic truck for a change," Marc said after a few calls. "I like Brian a lot; he's a good partner, but having to tech every call gets old after a while."

"I know what you mean," Bryan answered in his slow

southern drawl. "My partner's a Basic too," he said, referring to Mandy, his usual cohort. "She's been moved to dispatch."

"Oh yeah, I was wondering who that was on the radio. When is she due?" asked Marc.

"Not for six months. But her doctor said she had to be on light duty, so no lifting or CPR or anything. I've been working with mystery meat since she got moved. I worked with your partner on Wednesday. He said paramedic class is killing him. I said 'boy, you're preachin' to the choir here.' He'll make a good paramedic one day."

Both paramedics laughed at Brian's complaint about how difficult paramedic class was. Marc had been a paramedic for fifteen years and an EMT-Basic and an EMT-Intermediate for four years before that. Bryan had been a paramedic for five years and a Basic for two years. Yet both could recall their own difficulties with paramedic school as if it had been just last week.

They picked up a patient with continuous seizures, a kid with asthma, an elderly man who had fallen and broken his hip, and a overdose during the first half of the shift. All their patients had required interventions: IV's and oxygen on all of them, Valium for the seizure, Albuterol and Atrovent for the asthma, Morphine for the broken hip and Narcan for the overdose. "Man, we are some drug-pushing bitches today!" Bryan observed.

"No shit!" Marc responded. "I don't mind picking up patients that actually need the ambulance; it's those chronic motherfuckers that step on my last nerve with both feet."

"Oh, I know," Bryan answered. "I had Jimmy Givens the other day with your partner. Tried to tell me he hadn't been to the hospital in months when I knew full well that I had picked him up two weeks before that."

"You mean that guy who always tries to claim he was a Green Beret?"

"That's the one. If he was a Green Beret, then so was my grandmother. Fucking crackhead. And the worst part about him is he really does have medical problems, so you can't get him to refuse transport or tell him to get up the street," Bryan went on.

"And he cops an attitude when you try to call him out on his bullshit."

"Yeah, I know him," Marc affirmed, pondering the possibilities of Givens being his next recipient of his unique form of therapy.

After nightfall, the French Quarter calls began coming out as usual. Since it was Friday night, it was particularly busy. Mandy called Bryan and Marc to send them to a "man down" at 800 Bourbon Street, at the Oz.

"This is your neck of the woods!" Marc joked with Bryan as they drove to the scene.

Bryan smiled. "Nah, I never go there. Bunch of posers at the Oz. I like the Bourbon Pub across the street. Good music videos."

"Videos, huh? Riiiight," Marc kidded. He and Bryan both laughed at the irony of the joke. Bryan was a very good-looking, muscular man from backwoods Mississippi, the hunting/fishing/football type of guy. Even his name at work was a joke; Gay Bryan was one of the last people anyone would expect to be gay, even though he was "out" and it was no secret.

"They do have good videos," Bryan said, still laughing. Many of the EMT's, both gay and straight at the service, visited the Pub for drinks. Tolerance for "alternative lifestyles" in EMS was a non-issue. The unspoken camaraderie that existed between the EMT's drawn from the pressure of dealing with life, death and suffering day in and day out transcended any prejudice over being straight, gay, black, white or any other dividing line that others might recognize.

At the scene, there was a swirling crowd of people at the corner of Bourbon and St. Ann. Since it was near New Year's, the state had sent in extra state troopers to assist NOPD with law enforcement. Blue lights flashed all around, making the street a more flamboyant disco floor than the mirrored ball and lasers did inside the gay bar. Bryan pulled the stretcher out of the truck as Marc headed into the crowd to try to find their patient. Marc's search was unnecessary, as four state troopers pushed out of the mass of people toward the ambulance carrying a man by his arms and legs. Even before Bryan could lower the stretcher to ground level, the state police swung the unconscious man up and flopped him onto the stretcher.

"Wow. Thanks!" said Bryan, appreciative of the troopers' saving him and Marc the trouble of going through the crowd.

As he and Marc got the stretcher and the man back into the truck, two other men began to climb into the back of the truck, both wearing only tight jeans and leather harnesses over their bare chests despite the cold December night, the same outfit as the man on the stretcher. "We're physicians!" they both shouted. "He's in cardiac arrest!"

"Whoa, whoa! Y'all can't come up in here!" Marc shouted at them over the noise of the crowd and music pouring out of the nearby bars.

"We're both emergency room doctors! We work at the Air Force base in Biloxi! He's in cardiac arrest!"

Bryan had been assessing the patient and attaching the EKG monitor. "They're right, he is in cardiac arrest," he said noting the ventricular fibrillation on the monitor. Bryan began chest compressions. "You two can come, but you have to assume full responsibility for the patient and you have to ride with us to the hospital," Bryan informed the two of the service's policy for on-scene physicians who wanted to bark orders at the EMS crews.

The two guys looked at each other and hesitated a moment. Usually, informing a doctor of the policy was enough to scare the doctor away when faced with the inconvenience and liability of assuming care of whatever random patient they happened to find themselves near on 911 scenes.

"Okay, we'll go with you!" one said as they climbed into the truck.

"Oh, Jesus!" Bryan muttered under his breath to Marc.

"He needs to be defibrillated!" one of the doctors shouted, with a gay lisp that made both Marc and Bryan chuckle.

"I know," said Marc as he attached the defibrillator pads to the man's bare chest. "Well, that harness at least makes it easy to get to his chest," he commented nonchalantly.

"You can defibrillate?" the doctor said.

"Um, yeah. Clear," he said making sure no one was touching the man or the stretcher. He charged the monitor and hit the shock button.

"He needs to be intubated!" the other doctor shouted.

"I know," said Bryan. "I'm on it," he said as he pulled out a laryngoscope and endotracheal tube. He pushed the blade of the scope down the man's throat, followed by the tube.

"You can intubate?" the lispy doctor asked.

"Obviously. Check his breath sounds," he said to the physician, tossing him his stethoscope.

"You're in!" shouted the doctor, listening to the man's chest as Bryan squeezed the Ambu bag to ventilate the patient.

Marc had started an IV on the man while Bryan intubated. "He needs Epi!" the doctor lisped.

"Yes he does," Marc said calmly. "Got it right here." Marc pulled an Epinephrine syringe from the bag.

"You have Epi?" asked the doctor as Marc injected it into the IV.

It was Bryan's turn to handle the patient, and he was already getting tired of the screechy doctors in the back of truck with him. But he tried to remain professional while dealing with the physicians. "Okay, y'all, what are your names?"

"I'm Steve, this is Max," lisped Steve.

"Steve, Max, I appreciate your help, but let's try to keep the shouting down. Steve, you ventilate the patient. Max, you do chest compressions," Bryan gently ordered them.

Once the two doctors had something to do to keep them occupied, the code went much better. It left Marc and Bryan to perform their duties without shouting and hysteria in the back of the unit. The monitor still showed a crazy, uncoordinated line on the screen - ventricular fibrillation. Bryan charged the monitor and shocked the patient again. After a minute or two, he told Max to stop his compressions so a pulse could be checked. The monitor beeped with a coherent pattern now. Max and Bryan both felt for a pulse.

"He's got a pulse!" Max said, apparently surprised that an ambulance crew might possibly accomplish such a feat.

Bryan checked a blood pressure. "Seventy over thirty. Let's start some Dopamine."

Marc pulled out the Dopamine from the bag and hooked it into the IV line, setting the rate after a quick calculation in his head. "Time to go?" he asked Bryan.

Bryan nodded and keyed up his radio "Carry me to Tulane," he said, informing dispatch.

Marc exited the truck, casting a quick glance at the two leather-clad men, then at Bryan, offering a sympathetic smile as he closed the door. *'Poor guy. Having to deal with not one but two doctors! God help him,'* he thought.

Bryan cut off the man's jeans and fished around for identification in the pockets to help get information for the run report. Bryan noticed Max and Steve checking out the patient's naked crotch. "So do y'all know this guy?"

"No we had just met him. We were dancing with him and he collapsed," Max informed.

"Probably ecstasy or GHB or something," Bryan proffered. He noted the two physicians giving each other worried looks at the mention of illegal recreational drugs. *'Yeah, that's what I thought. Whatever; who cares?'* Bryan thought to himself.

The patient maintained a pulse on the way to the hospital and the Dopamine increased his blood pressure to normal levels. By the time they arrived, the man had begun moving a little bit on his own, a sign of a successful resuscitation. Bryan and Marc rolled the patient into the ER trailed by Max and Steve in their tight jeans, construction boots and leather harnesses strapped across their bare chests. Both paramedics had a hard time controlling their laughter at the looks the ER staff was giving the two leather-daddy doctors.

After giving his report to the staff, Steve told Marc and Bryan "You two were great. I wish codes would go that well in the hospital!"

"Thanks. Y'all can come ride with us whenever you like," Bryan responded, subtly eyeing Steve and Max up and down.

Marc caught the almost imperceptible motion of Bryan's eyes and could hold onto his laughter no longer. He began laughing so hard he fell onto the ground outside on the ER ramp. All three gay guys knew exactly what Marc found so funny and they too began their own bouts of uncontrolled laughing, having been caught cruising each other while trying to maintain some semblance of professionalism while wearing their ridiculous outfits.

"Dude, that was hilarious!" Marc told Bryan later in the truck. Both medics would have a case of the giggles for a while to come, spontaneously bursting out chuckling when thinking about the insane circumstances surrounding their patient. It was situations like that that made for a "good call."

They had a short break until their next call. It was for a man with "chest pains." Marc wrote down the address as Bryan drove. "I'll bet this is our friend," Marc informed.

"I thought that address sounded familiar. Good ol' Jimmy again. Wonder how long we'll be on scene before he says something about being a Green Beret," Bryan commented.

Bryan didn't have to wonder long. As they pulled up on scene, Jimmy Givens met them at the street, wearing a baseball cap, tee shirt and jacket, all three garments emblazoned with "Green Beret" on them. He actually wore a lime-colored beret, one that still had the price tag from the thrift store Jimmy had purchased or stolen the clothes.

Marc rolled down the window as Jimmy walked up to the truck. "What's up Jimmy?"

"Man, I need to go the hospital. My chest is killing me," Jimmy explained.

"Jimmy, I just brought you there two days ago for the same

thing," Bryan said from the driver's seat.

"What, you tellin' me I ain't having no chest pains? Man, I protect and serve you and this country every damn day and you're saying I ain't sick? I'm a damn Green Beret, man!"

"Protect and serve us, huh? How? By calling 911 every day for your non-existent chest pain?" Bryan argued back.

Marc decided to end the bickering. "Come on, Jimmy, get in the truck," he said, getting out and opening the back door for Jimmy. Bryan grumped and hopped into the back too.

On the stretcher, Jimmy continued complaining about the paramedic's attitude towards him. Both Marc and Bryan knew he complained about EMS crews' "attitudes" regardless of how polite the crews were, so it made no difference whether they were polite or insulting.

Bryan attached the monitor and ran a twelve-lead EKG while Marc checked a blood pressure. The EKG was a mess, as usual. Givens had a litany of real medical problems, many brought on by his constant crack abuse. Marc listened through his stethoscope to the blood pressure. "Seventy-two over fifty," he informed Bryan. "I think he really has something going on today."

"You see? I told you I was sick!" Jimmy told Bryan with venom in his voice.

Marc looked for a vein in Jimmy's arm to start an IV on while Bryan spiked a bag of IV fluid. "I'm not gonna fish around; you've got no veins I can see here. I'm going to have to stick you in your neck, Jimmy."

"Yeah, you do that. I serve you every day; it's about time you serve me," Jimmy ordered.

Marc laid the stretcher down and stuck the needle into the jugular vein on the right side of Jimmy's neck and attached the IV line. "Just run it wide open," he told Bryan. "Pull out the Dopamine, I'll give it en route."

Bryan opened the bag and located the spare Dopamine. They had used the premixed bag on their cardiac arrest earlier, so Marc would have to prepare and mix the vials of undiluted Dopamine. Bryan pulled out the two vials of the drug and a smaller IV bag of D5W, 5% Dextrose in water. He placed it on the bench seat and hopped out to get back into the driver's seat. *'I'm glad it's Marc's turn. I can't stand that bastard. I'd be tempted to just give him all the Dopamine at once,"* Bryan thought to himself.

Marc drew up the Dopamine into a syringe and stuck a piece of tape on the IV bag, writing "Dopamine 400 mg" on it so it would be clearly labeled. He spiked the bag and piggybacked the line onto the first IV going into Jimmy's neck.

"That asshole thinks he can talk to me like that. I'll sue his ass! I'm a Green Beret and he ain't shit!" complained Jimmy about Bryan as the ambulance headed off.

Marc picked up the syringe full of undiluted Dopamine. It was used to increase blood pressure. Jimmy's run report would say his pressure had initially been 72/50. Marc calculated the proper infusion rate for Jimmy. Jimmy should get ten micrograms per kilogram of body weight per minute. His calculation came up with an infusion of a half-milliliter of IV solution per minute, eight hundred micrograms of Dopamine per minute to increase his blood pressure with the powerful medication. Marc would need all this information for his report later, but not now. He injected the syringe of pure Dopamine directly into the IV line, giving Jimmy over five hundred times that amount in the space of one second.

Marc pictured the cells in Jimmy's body. Dopamine was a natural chemical found in the body. It functioned as a neurotransmitter and helped regulate blood pressure and brain activity. When given as a medication, extremely tiny amounts were used. Marc envisioned the neural receptors in Jimmy's heart. Suddenly flooded with pure dopamine, they would contract and not relax. The EKG monitor confirmed Marc's imagination. It showed a brief interval of ventricular fibrillation, then a flat line a few seconds later as the Dopamine washed over the cardiac muscle cells. Some Dopamine reached Jimmy's brain and other organs in the final few heartbeats before all activity stopped. Marc imagined his brain cells being overwhelmed with the chemical. The overstimulation would cause a seizure, but being hypersaturated with Dopamine like Jimmy's heart, the synapses were unable to transmit the chemical messages through the nervous system to the body. As Marc had seen in his mind, Jimmy's body simply ceased to function.

Bryan was listening to his radio as he drove. He heard someone key up and announce to dispatch that their patient had just coded. It took a second for him to realize that the voice on the radio was that of his partner. "Givens coded?" he called through the window into the back.

"Yep. Went into asystole," Marc informed.

"Holy shit! That's awesome! I'll drive slow," Bryan responded, welcoming the unexpected news. *'I never thought we'd be rid of that bastard.'* he thought.

Marc began his usual steps. They were only a few minutes from the hospital, giving Marc time only to intubate Givens and push one round of Epinephrine and Atropine. He was about to shoot the drugs into the wheel well, but paused and gave them intravenously. The activity of the vasopressors would increase the action of the Dopamine that was inhibiting the function of the cells, ensuring that Givens wouldn't be resuscitated at the hospital.

The ER staff continued working on him, giving more Epinephrine and Atropine. Marc knew that every injection on top of all that Dopamine was pushing Jimmy farther and farther into the grave as his cells continued to be more and more overwhelmed. Each chest compression circulated the deluge of Dopamine throughout the body, shutting down organ systems one by one. The code drugs would come right behind and reinforce the overstimulation that the Dopamine had caused. After twenty minutes, Dr. Morgan decided to call it. "Time of death, twenty-two thirty-two," he announced.

Marc thought back to his church call from the previous Sunday. Givens had been weighed in Marc's balances and had been found wanting. He was a useless, lying, rude, crackhead thief, who had never served in the military a day in his life. He drew welfare, disability and Medicaid for the host of medical problems he had caused to himself. And Marc had no need to hide anything this time. He couldn't have asked for better circumstances. The Dopamine was clearly indicated to use for Givens low blood pressure, even though Marc had actually measured the pressure at a hundred ninety over ninety-four. What mattered was that is appeared on the run report as dangerously low, as Marc had misinformed Bryan. No one would check whether or not there really was Dopamine in the bag of fluid labeled "Dopamine 400 mg." And being a natural neurotransmitter, nothing unusual would show up in any autopsy, especially since the chemical would break down by the time an autopsy took place. Even the problem of tissue necrosis was solved. Such a huge dose of Dopamine would normally result in tissue death if it had been injected in an IV in an arm, but since the IV was basically a central line, placed into the large jugular vein, nothing would be noticeable. It was perfect.

Marc and Gay Bryan finished out their shift, transporting one more patient to the hospital, a gunshot victim shot to the chest. After work, Bryan asked Marc if he wanted to go for a drink. Marc accepted, asking "Where do you wanna go?"

Bryan answered "Where do you think? Bourbon and St. Ann! Let's go find those doctors."

Marc laughed again. "Okay, man. Sure."

They headed out and found Max and Steve, hung out at the Bourbon Pub till four a.m, exchanged stories and recollected the events from earlier, as EMT's usually did when away from work. Eventually, Bryan left with the two doctors; Marc headed home.

'This was a good day,' he thought to himself as he laid down to sleep.

Sunday rolled around; Marc's next scheduled day to work. Straight Brian was back. He greeted Marc as he got the truck ready for the day. On the way out of the station, Brian commented "I heard you coded what's-his-name, that Green Beret guy who always calls. Bryan was telling me"

"Yeah," answered Marc. "Died right in the back of the truck

on the way to the hospital."

"Hmm," he said. "Another one like that?" Brian thought for a few minutes as an odd silence filled the truck. "I have to ask you something."

Chapter 10

"What's that?" Marc asked as they pulled into the convenience store to get their usual morning cup of coffee.

"Let's get our coffee," answered Brian. He had been thinking about the empty vial of potassium chloride he had found. He had gotten distracted since his shift with Joyce; dealing with paramedic class, calling in sick, recuperating from a rough week. After a few days he had nearly forgotten about the unusual medication he had found in the sharps box when it accidentally spilled out. He gave it a minute and waited till after obtaining their drinks and were back in the truck.

"Ever heard of potassium chloride?" he asked Marc.

"Of course," Marc replied, somewhat less cheerful. "Why?"

"What's it used for?" Brian inquired.

"For patients with hypokalemia. Low blood potassium can result in arrhythmias. It usually looks like a tall T-wave on the EKG. If your potassium's really low, it can kill you. Studying pharmacology this week, I see," he answered, laughing but without humor.

"I was looking up drugs on the internet. Potassium can be quite deadly, apparently," Brian said. "Did you know it's also the stuff they use on Death Row for executions by lethal injection?" Brian continued.

"Yes. Too much potassium will kill you the same as not enough." Marc fidgeted in his seat. "Why do you ask?"

"Do we carry it on the truck?"

"No. It has to be given on a pump and it's only given in the hospital," Marc answered flatly, looking straight out the front of the windshield. He paused a second and asked Brian "Did you bring your lunch today or are we buying lunch today?"

"I'll have to stop and get something. Or try to, at least," Brian answered. Just as he opened his mouth to change the subject back, dispatch called on the radio, "Stand by to copy," said Mandy.

Mandy dispatched Marc and Brian to a motor vehicle accident on the West Bank. Behrman and Tullis, almost at the Jefferson Parish line. "One of the vehicles is supposedly on fire, I'm sending rescue and fire with you," she said.

Brian wrote down the information and rolled his eyes. "You ever notice how the more hysterical dispatch sounds about calls, the less serious the calls are?" he noted.

Marc laughed more genuinely as he drove to the scene. "Yep. Guarantee you this'll be nothing but a bunch of bullshit," he commented.

They pulled up to the intersection. Both medics quickly surveyed the scene and were astonished that it really did appear to be a serious accident. One car was near the side of the road, upright but it had obviously rolled over several times. The only undamaged portion of it was one of the tires that wasn't flat. The other car was across the street lying on its side, its front end still wrapped around the stump of the telephone pole it had broken. Flames licked out from under the hood. Bystanders had gathered around the car and appeared to be pulling the car's occupant out of the open sunroof.

Marc looked at the upright car on his left and noted two occupants inside, not moving, apparently dead. "I'll look at this car, they're gonna be fatalities. You take the other one."

Brian ran over to the burning car and enlisted the bystanders to help move the female farther away from the burning vehicle. She appeared dead, with burns over much of her body and several fractures apparent.

Marc peered into the upright car and saw the two women inside, not breathing. Their bodies were pushed up into the center of the car and the mass of wreckage around them made it impossible for him to reach them. "Keep rescue coming, but this is gonna be a recovery; I have at least two fatalities here." He glanced over at Brian across the street and saw a dangerous situation; Marc couldn't waste any time by walking over to the other car. "Brian, get those bystanders out from under that power line!" he called to his partner over his radio. "The pole is broken and the car is setting fire to it!"

Brian glanced up, saw the power lines hanging awkwardly and evacuated the bystanders from the area. Marc had arrived with the EKG monitor. He told Brian to help him move her farther from the burning car. As he attached the monitor, he saw the display confirm the burned woman was dead. The flames from the nearby car began to spread from under the hood to the rest of the car. "Get out from under these power lines," he ordered Brian. He contacted medical control quickly to get the woman pronounced dead. Halfway through his report, the flaming car exploded; Marc felt the heat and the blast but was distant enough that he was uninjured. The broken pole had caught fire; Marc decided it was time to get away and headed back to the first car. As he left, another explosion emanated from the burning car, knocking the pole and breaking the power lines, which sparked and crackled on the ground in the exact spot that Marc, Brian and the bystanders had been. Marc completed his report and obtained a time of death, switched back to the dispatch channel and asked for the power company to come out to disable the electricity. "We don't need any electrocutions on top of all this mess," he informed.

Marc tried to get Do Not Resuscitate orders on the other two women in the first car. "I have two patients in this car, both females approximately in their mid-twenties, unresponsive and apneic. The vehicle is too damaged for me to climb in and get an EKG on them or do any kind of interventions, but their injuries are apparently incompatible with life, and it's gonna be a very extended extrication process to get them out. Calling for DNR."

Dr. Hunter on the other end of the radio said "So can you give me an idea of what kind of injuries they have? Are you sure they're pulseless?"

Marc repeated "As I said, I can't really physically get to them, so I can't give you a full assessment of their injuries. But I can tell you that both are unresponsive and not breathing, crushed under several feet of car, so whatever their specific injuries are was enough to cause death. Calling for DNR on both."

"Well, I'm not going to be able to pronounce them until I have a better assessment. Is there any way you can get closer to assess them?" Dr. Hunter asked.

Marc glanced at Ricky, the rescue paramedic who had arrived on the scene in the extrication truck. "Is he giving you shit trying to get a DNR?" Ricky asked, confounded that Marc was getting such a hard time from medical control.

"Yeah! Wants me to get a better assessment! I can't get anywhere close to those women unless you cut the whole car apart! What the hell?" Marc said to Ricky, almost exasperated.

Brian shouted to Marc from a hundred yards away, "Marc! We have another patient! She's alive!"

"Shit!" Marc said. He keyed up his radio but released the button, not knowing what else to say to Dr. Hunter. He was obviously not going to grant a DNR on the other two dead patients, and now Marc had someone who had survived the accident to deal with. Marc knew the new patient's injuries would be severe, judging from the impact that was enough to kill three other people.

Ricky noted Marc's quandary. "Dude, you go deal with the new patient; I'll handle this and get your DNR from med control. You have bigger fish to fry," Ricky said, switching over to the medical control channel to talk to Dr. Hunter.

"Thanks, man. I owe you one," Marc said, taking him up on his offer. Marc grabbed a spineboard and cervical collar from the truck and headed over to Brian's location.

The woman was unconscious; bystanders had gotten her out of the burning vehicle first, and told Brian about her while Marc was dealing with medical control. She had a head injury and red marks on her chest. The two medics quickly got her onto the board and collar and into the truck. "Blood pressure is eighty-six over forty, heart rate one-thirty, pulseox is 75%" Brian informed.

Marc attached the EKG leads and spiked a bag of IV fluid. "Check her breath sounds," he said to Brian.

Brian listened to her chest through his stethoscope. "I dunno, I think they're okay. She's not really taking deep breaths."

"All right, you get this IV, I'll check," he said.

After observing and listening to her chest, Marc fished the airway supplies out of the bag. "She's got a tension pneumo; have you ever decompressed a chest before?"

"No," Brian answered, nervousness in his voice. "You mean like a chest tube? We have those?"

"No," answered Marc. "We just have to make do." He located a fourteen gauge IV needle from the bag and attached a syringe to the end of it. Brian watched as Marc swabbed the left side of the girl's chest with alcohol, then pushed the needle deep into it, near her left shoulder. Brian winced as he watched Marc stab her. He pushed the IV needle in, pulled the plunger back on the syringe, withdrawing air and a little frothy blood, then took the needle out, leaving the IV catheter protruding from the chest, which hissed as the needle came out.

"Dude, you got that IV started?" he asked Brian, who had gotten distracted from the task while watching Marc perform the chest decompression.

"Oh, sorry!" he answered. He turned back to the arm he was trying to start the IV on.

Marc pulled out the laryngoscope and an endotracheal tube. The cervical collar made it difficult to open the girl's mouth enough to see, and she gagged as the steel blade pressed deep in her throat.

"Man, how are you gonna intubate her? She's still breathing and..."

Marc waited a second for her to inhale and as she did, he pushed the tube into her trachea and inflated the cuff to hold it in place before Brian could finish his sentence.

He attached the Ambu bag and listened to the chest with his stethoscope to make sure the tube was in the right place. "You were saying?" he asked Brian, smiling. "Breath sounds are better; what's her pulseox?"

"Up to ninety-three percent!" Brian said, obviously impressed with Marc's skills. He had been on many trauma calls with Marc and knew he was a skilled paramedic, but watching him in action on such a stressful call impressed Brian even more deeply. "Ready to hit the road?" Brian asked.

"Yep," he said.

On the way to the hospital, Brian reviewed the scene in his head. He had been overwhelmed at the accident, unsure what to do besides help pull the body from the burning car. The danger of the burning power lines had escaped his notice, but not Marc's; he had saved Brian and the bystanders from electrocution. There were three fatalities to deal with, and Marc had done so efficiently and emotionlessly, even while the medical control doctor was making an already difficult scene even worse. Marc worked quickly and skillfully on the injured girl, recognized the life-threatening injury that Brian had missed and managed to complete interventions that Brian doubted he could have done himself. Despite the fatalities, Marc had saved lives today, and not just the patient on the stretcher.

After delivering the girl to the hospital, Brian asked about her. "How could you tell she had a tension pneumothorax? I checked her breath sounds and they sounded fine."

"You may have heard the crepitus, the noise from her fractured ribs moving, but she had no breath sounds on the left. And her trachea was deviated, and there was some JVD too. Classic signs of a tension pneumo."

Brian felt sheepish. He knew he was a good EMT and had some the best grades in his paramedic class. But he felt embarrassed that he had been unable to properly assess the girl. Marc had assessed her, decompressed her chest and gotten her intubated in two or three minutes. Brian was still flailing around trying to get one IV while Marc did all that. "Good job," he told

Marc, feeling somewhat deflated.

"Thanks," Marc answered, putting his arm across Brian's shoulder as they walked back to the ambulance. "You'll get the hang of it with experience. You did well too. You were about to ask me something before this call. What were we talking about?"

"Oh. Yeah. Um... I was asking you about potassium."

Marc quit smiling, abruptly knocked down from his adrenaline high. "Oh. Okay," he said with a completely different tone in his voice.

Brian was not even sure he wanted to bring up the subject again, especially after seeing how proficiently Marc had acted on the scene of the accident. *'Surely there can't be anything amiss. I must have been crazy to think that anything unusual was going on with Marc,'* Brian thought. But Marc's sudden change in demeanor set off the strange alert in his head again. *'Do you think your partner did something that caused them to die?'* he recalled Tammy's words from months before.

A flood of suspicion entered Brian's mind at that point. The unusual deaths, the potassium he found, Tammy's ideas of foul play, Marc's sudden change in mood at the mention of the potassium - all coalesced into a dark picture that formed in Brian's head. Another awkward silence filled the truck as these thoughts overwhelmed Brian. Finally, one more image entered his mind. He pictured Marc kneeling on the floor of the church they responded to last week, uttering the words of the preacher, *'you have been weighed in the balances and you have been found wanting.'* All the strange deaths had been people that they had discussed as being not worthy of existence, a burden on society. *'Is Marc killing the people that he thinks aren't worthy of existence?'*

"You said it's used for patients with hypokalemia?" Brian finally said.

"Yes."

"And what do you use it for?" Brian asked, not quite able to make eye contact with Marc.

He turned slowly to Brian. *'What the fuck?'* Marc thought to himself. *'How does he know? Every time it's been perfect, with no evidence. How do I answer this?'*

"What makes you think I use potassium?" he said after a long pause.

"Marc, I found an empty vial of potassium in the truck. We're the only ones that have used this truck in weeks. You had to have put it there. I didn't. What was it doing there?" he asked as calmly as he could. Brian kept thinking as he spoke *'He didn't deny using potassium. Please give me a legitimate reason for it's being there.'*

Marc stammered on his words. "It... I... I have no idea how it got in the sharps box. Someone else must have put it there."

Brian was horrified. His eyes grew wide and his breaths came fast. "Marc, I never said it was in the sharps box."

Both medics sat silently, their heads against the seat, staring at the ceiling. Both quietly confronted their worst fears. Marc had been discovered killing patients. Brian was accusing his partner of murder and had found out he was right. Neither knew what to say.

"Stand by to copy," said Mandy over the radio. No matter how serious or stupid this call was, both EMT's felt relief at the distraction this call would offer. They drove to the scene to handle the call. Both medics knew that handling the 911 calls came first and this issue would have to be dealt with in the midst of emergency responses. Their discussion continued throughout the day and night, broken up by responses to calls. They spoke about it on scenes, in the back of the truck and over patients they were treating.

"Why do you do it? Does it have something to do with that 'weighed in the balance' thing I heard you quote at the church last week?" Brian asked as Marc pushed Narcan into the IV of an overdose patient.

Marc pondered a moment, trying to phrase his words correctly. "I think you already know why. You, yourself, said 'why are we keeping him alive?' when we picked up Johannes one day. Tell me, why did you say that?

Brian saw where Marc's line of reasoning was going. "Because he was a useless oxygen thief. He burdened EMS every day with his drunkenness." Brian admitted. As the overdose woke up, the conversation was suspended till the next opportune moment.

"Right. Not only did Johannes burden us, but every hospital in the city. And who pays for all those ER visits?" Marc asked while tying four-point restraints to a combative, postictal seizure patient.

Brian thought for a minute while keeping the patient's arms restrained from punching him again. "We do."

"And what did Johannes contribute to society?" Marc asked. "What did we... I mean, the world, gain from his being alive?"

Brian didn't know what to say. He just stared as Marc squirted Versed into the patient's nostril to calm him down. '*I'd like some Versed too. I wish I'd never brought it up,*' he thought.

"But you can't just go around killing people!" Brian almost shouted. "It's... illegal!"

"No, you can't kill people!" said the ninety year-old on the stretcher in a brief moment of clarity from his Alzheimer's delirium.

"Just because allowing the parasites of society to live is legal, doesn't mean it's *right.*" Marc said sincerely.

Brian was confused. "What?"

"Abortion is legal; does that mean it's right? Stem cell therapy is illegal; does that mean it's wrong? When a rapist or child molester gets off scot-free on a legal technicality, is that right?"

"But we're here to save lives, not kill people," Brian protested. "How can that be right?"

Marc secured the cervical collar as Brian strapped the mentally retarded Down's Syndrome patient to the spineboard. He shrieked and thrashed in fright, making it difficult for the medics to avoid getting spattered with blood from his lacerated head. "Take a look at the rest of the world," Marc said. "Do wild animals tolerate other animals who contribute nothing to the pack? A tiger that refuses to hunt dies. A squirrel that doesn't store food for the winter starves. Whole ecosystems have evolved to eliminate parasites - cleaner fish and cowbirds; they exist by removing parasites and the other animals line up to receive their services."

Marc motioned to the Down's Syndrome man screaming on the spineboard. "Do you think that this poor soul would have lived to adulthood in any other society? He would have been eaten by the wolves long ago. But at least having Down's isn't his fault, he can't help it."

"So why not do one of your mercy killings to him, seeing as he's so useless?" Brian asked sullenly.

"He's not useless, that's the thing. We picked him up from his job. He works at that broom factory making brooms. Sure it's not much, but he contributes something to the world. Just because you're handicapped doesn't mean you're useless. Ever heard of Steven Hawking? Can't move a muscle, he's paralyzed in a wheelchair from Lou Gehrig's Disease. He's also one of the greatest physicists in the world." Marc explained. "I don't care if you're handicapped or perfectly healthy, I just need to know if you even *want* to be a productive human being. Think of Johannes, did he even try to do anything with his life anymore?"

Brian thought for a long while. "I don't know. How can you set yourself up to be judge and executioner of these people? No, I'm not going to kiss you," he said as the drunken sorority girl on the stretcher continued to ask the medics to make out with her.

"We all judge. Some people judge others based on first impressions. Some people judge others based on their race or nationality or religion or sexual orientation. Stop, you're getting vomit on me," Marc said as he removed the drunken girl's hand from his crotch. "I'm only taking action against behavior that everyone else complains about, but they do nothing to rectify it. Even you've told me that you wondered why we tolerate parasites."

"Yeah, but I don't kill them!" he argued.

"Like I said, just because it's legal, doesn't mean it's right - letting the parasites live," Marc answered. "Instead of taking an example from nature, which by the way, has prospered for billions of years by 'survival of the fittest,' people have set up a system that allows individuals to leech off of others their whole lives, sucking up resources but never contributing a thing to the system that supports them."

"So that's your criteria? Whether or not someone has a job and pays taxes?" Brian asked as he started an IV on the gunshot victim.

"Not necessarily. You can be a productive human being without a job. For example, someone who's jobless and on welfare can still raise a decent family. A poor starving artist who doesn't pay taxes is still contributing something to the world."

As a vial of crack cocaine fell out from between the patient's butt cheeks after Marc had cut off his pants, Brian asked "So what about this guy? He's a drug dealer, not contributing to society. Why are you bothering to help him?"

"His lifestyle will kill him. Hell, it already has. He's not going to survive this," Marc said, pointing at the brain tissue protruding from the hole in his head. "He doesn't need me to help with that."

Marc applied an oxygen mask to the unconscious priest who was having a stroke. "Everyone needs to have a function in the world. Mine is like the cleaner fish and birds. I help society by getting rid of those who unnecessarily burden and sicken the rest of the population."

Brian said little through the rest of the shift, thinking about Marc's arguments. *'He's so damned logical about it, but he can't be right. Killing people cannot be right, no matter how you look at it,'* he thought.

After their shift was over, they stood in the station parking lot together. Marc smoked a cigarette; Brian stared at the ground. "Can I ask how many?" Brian said, his eyes fixed on the pavement.

"I have no reason to lie to you. Eleven," he said. "So now that you know, what are you going to do about it?" Marc asked Brian, depression in his tone.

The cardinal rule of EMS sounded in Brian's head. *'What happens in the truck, stays in the truck. But I can't just let this slide! Knowing about it makes me an accomplice!'*

"I don't know, man," Brian said at last. "I'll have to think about it. This is a lot to deal with."

"Making the world a better place is never easy, and seldom welcomed. You do whatever you think you have to do." Marc got into his pickup and drove away, leaving Brian lost in thought. After a minute, Brian drove away too. In each of their cars, both medics cried.

Chapter 11

Brian had stopped crying by the time he got home. He was worried Tammy might have decided to stay over and he didn't want her to see him bawling; he didn't want to tell anyone yet what he now knew. After getting undressed and showering, he took a beer from the fridge and sat down in front of the TV with the remote in his hand. An hour later, the TV was still off, the beer warm and flat. He realized he had been sitting there thinking about Marc the whole time.

He carefully considered what Marc had said. They had talked about Johannes; Brian thought about him too. *'This dude's about as useful as the garbage on the street he lays in,'* were Brian's own words describing Johannes. He thought about the dialysis patient who had mysteriously died while en route to the hospital. He had done nothing for himself; he forced everyone around him to take care of him. He didn't even bother taking his medications. He had picked up Jimmy Givens three times with Marc. It was apparent that Givens was never a Green Beret; but rather a crackhead who existed by stealing. Brian also couldn't ignore the fact that Marc was a great paramedic. He had seen him save many lives. Today, Marc had saved Brian's own life too. Marc had found his calling in EMS.

'No!' Brian shook himself out of his absorption. *'I am not going to be sucked into that line of reasoning! No matter how non-productive a person is, they're still a person. It can never be right to kill anyone, no matter how you judge them in your "balances." I have to tell someone about this; it can't be right no matter how well Marc tries to justify it.'*

He thought about the oath he took upon becoming an EMT. Similar to the Hippocratic Oath that doctors took, it stated that he would "abstain from whatever is deleterious." Marc took that oath too. But Marc was convinced that what he was doing was not deleterious. He viewed himself as a helper of humanity by eliminating "deleterious" aspects of society.

'Stop, damn it!' Brian chided himself as he considered Marc's words again. He decided to quit thinking about it and try to sleep. He slept fitfully, tossing and turning through most of the night. On the occasions he actually was asleep, he dreamt of white birds on the back of a rhinoceros, picking ticks off. The birds kept picking and picking until they had consumed the entire rhino. The birds flew off, emanating the sound of a siren. Brian woke, hearing the sound of a real siren fading past his window. *'This is gonna be a long night.'*

Marc fared no better. He and Brian weren't scheduled to be back at work for two days, so he had the entire two days to torture himself. He imagined what prison would be like. He had been to Orleans Parish Prison many times to pick up patients and there were no tolerable aspects of the facility. *'Maybe I could just deny it if Brian chooses to tell anyone. After all, there's no evidence. All those patients died from "natural causes" brought on by their own health problems. If there are any autopsy reports, they just show there was hyperkalemia, or drug abuse or head injuries or whatever. I could say that he's just being paranoid; that the stress of the streets and school is getting to him. That maybe EMS isn't the career for him.'*

That thought depressed Marc too. Brian really was a good EMT and he would be a fine paramedic eventually. Plus he liked Brian; he considered him his friend. He didn't want to destroy Brian's life and career in an effort to protect his own. Marc poured himself some bourbon, quaffed it down, then poured another and another, until he was blistering drunk. Finally he passed out on his bed. He dreamed he was sitting on the back bumper of the ambulance banging his clipboard against his head until the clipboard was bloody and bent. He woke up from his drunken binge in mid-afternoon, his head feeling exactly like it had been beaten with his metal clipboard. Marc had finished off his bourbon the night before, so he poured some orange juice and vodka and spent the rest of that day drunk too.

Marc woke up before the alarm clock. His head continued to pound. He had a couple of hours before reporting to work. *'Will this be my last day?'* he wondered. He didn't want to face this day hungover. Marc searched through the medical equipment that had followed him home from work over time. Every EMT has a pile of stuff off the ambulance for their own emergency use, and Marc was no exception. He spiked a bag of Lactated Ringer's solution and started an IV on himself. A liter or two of IV fluid was the best cure for a hangover. He added a half a syringe of IV Dextrose to the bag and an ampule of Thiamine. It was a recipe that had worked many times on Marc and the other EMT's when they had lingered too long at the bar after work. When the IV had drained, he spiked a second bag of fluid and let that infuse as well. After an hour or so, he felt great.

'Let's see how long I feel good,' he thought as he donned his uniform. At the station, he saw Brian walking from his car to clock in. Marc put his gear in the truck; so did Brian. They checked out the inventory, oil, transmission fluid; the entire time neither said a word to each other or even made eye contact. Eventually it was time to go on duty. Both avoided the elephant in the room and sat silently as they drove to get their morning coffee, still not even looking at each other.

They were sent to cover New Orleans East. It was a slow day, and both medics wished for a call to have something to do besides try to ignore each other. Marc eventually could take it no longer. "Well? I guess you've had some time to think of our last conversation."

Brian sighed. "Yes. Marc, I can't let this happen. You can't just go around killing people just because you think they're a drain on the rest of us. Murdering the people who piss you off doesn't eliminate the problem."

"What do you mean? You're going to turn me in?" Marc asked. "I've been thinking about it too, and it occurs to me that there's no evidence to back you up if you were to make such a claim. You know I can always say that you just weren't cut out for this job; that you can't handle the fact that sometimes people just die in the truck. I've been working here almost as long as you've been alive! Who do you think they're going to believe?" he said, now fully on the defense.

Brian slumped back into the driver's seat. "I hadn't thought of that," he said, feeling defeated. He was so preoccupied with trying to figure out what to do, he never paused to realize that Marc might have been doing the same thing. His anger burned that Marc had placed him in this predicament. He fumed at Marc, and thought about putting themselves out of service and calling the supervisor to ask to be put in another truck with a different partner.

Finally, dispatch called them to respond to a scene. "An eight-year old with a vaginal bleed," said Hope over the radio. Brian drove, Marc stared out the window. He tried to change the subject. "This address sounds familiar. Do you recognize it? Maybe a frequent flier?" Marc asked.

Brian was still steaming. "I don't know. If it is, are you going to kill them?" he responded viciously.

"Look, you goddamn asshole, I'm sorry you're in this position, but you're the one who brought it up!" Marc shouted back, seething at Brian. "You couldn't just leave well enough alone! You had to push it after you dug through the fucking sharps container. What happens in the truck STAYS IN THE GODDAMNED FUCKING TRUCK!"

"Not this time, motherfucker! I was thinking about not reporting you to anyone, but so help me, I will see to it that you rot in fucking jail!" Brian shouted back.

"Really? We'll see about that. You're still on probation and I'll make sure you never set foot on one of these ambulances again! Suck on that for a while," Marc said angrily.

They turned onto the street where the address was. Both EMT's tried to stifle their emotions and put on a somewhat professional front to deal with the patient, even though both wanted to slug the other one in the jaw. "This is probably some eight-year old who got her period early. These idiots can't recognize a normal biological function if it bit them in the face," commented Marc, transferring his anger at Brian to the

108

prospective patient and her family.

"Damn, what the hell is going on here?" Brian said as he approached the address. Six police cars were out front of the house. Several officers were interviewing people in the front yard.

As they exited the truck, one of the cops pulled Brian and Marc aside before they walked in. "The little girl was raped. We just want you to make sure she doesn't have any life-threatening injuries; the rape squad is going to handle it and take her to the hospital for the exam."

"Oh, shit. How old?" Brian asked, his anger at Marc momentarily forgotten.

"Eight," said the policeman.

Marc closed his eyes, nauseated at the thought. Brian was likewise sickened. Both medics found a subconscious place where their feelings met in sorrow for the child. They turned and looked briefly at each other, realizing that despite their argument on the way to the scene, they both still felt compassion.

The house looked strangely familiar. "I have a weird *déjà-vu* going on right now," Marc whispered to Brian.

"We have been here before," Brian observed. "We coded an old lady here a while back," he said as they entered the very bedroom where they had done CPR on an elderly grandmother.

There were two cops and two other adults next to the bed. As Marc announced his presence, the adults moved aside to allow Marc to examine the patient. As they moved out of the way, Marc and Brian instantly recognized the frilly pink dress the little girl was wearing. There were only a few sparkly barrettes in her hair now, but Marc was transported to the last conversation he had had with this same girl. *'"Thank you for trying to save my grandma, mister. You did all you could, but I know she's in a better place now." "You're welcome, darling. I'm so sorry I couldn't do more."'*

Marc gasped when he recognized her. "Hi, sweetheart. Are you okay?" he asked, kneeling down so he was below her eye level.

The girl looked at him and appeared to recognize him, but said nothing. She was far from okay, but didn't know what to do or say.

Before touching her, Marc gently said "I'm going to try to help you, okay? Does anything hurt?"

The girl responded wordlessly. She nodded and touched her groin.

"I see. What's your name? I'm Marc," he said softly.

"Tamara," she said in a tiny, frightened voice.

"Tamara, I just need to check that you're not badly hurt, okay? I need to look where you're hurting, and the police will be able to help you. Is that all right?" Marc said with his eyes locked on hers, in a way that made Tamara feel like their conversation was completely private, as if there were no one else in the room.

Even Brian felt like an outsider from the way Marc spoke to the girl. He realized he had a function too and likewise knelt down next to Tamara.

"Okay," she told Marc, fear still in her voice.

Marc moved his hands slowly to lift up the girl's dress. She backed higher onto the bed, afraid that whatever Marc was going to do would hurt her more.

"Tamara, it's okay. I'm only going to look. I promise I won't do anything that hurts. You know you can trust me; I tried to help your grandmother, remember?"

Tamara relaxed just a little. She pulled her pink dress up just above her waist. Her underwear was torn and there were trickles of blood on her thighs. Marc pulled the elastic band on her panties just enough for him and Brian to peer inside for a few seconds. The girl's tiny labia were bruised and her hymen was torn. A drop of blood fell out into the underwear. Marc removed his hand from near the girl's privates.

"That's it, Tamara. I'm done. See? I promised I wouldn't hurt you," Marc said.

Like the last time they had met, the girl threw her arms around Marc. This time she hugged him again as hard as her little arms could muster. "Thank you, mister," she said, crying.

"You'll be all right," Brian said, his voice cracking. As the words left his mouth, he felt his words were completely inadequate. The girl looked at Brian and gave him a smile also, but her facial expression to Marc had engendered trust, whereas the look she gave to Brian made him feel as if she had done him a favor by acknowledging his presence.

Marc grasped her hand gently and said "I'm going to go now, but the policemen and your parents will help you now. Okay?"

Tamara nodded. Marc and Brian stood back up and headed out the house. Marc glanced at the girl's father, who months ago had managed to remain composed at his mother's death. He now stood in the corner of the bedroom, tears streaming from his eyes.

Brian thought to himself *'I have to hand it to Marc, he can handle tough scenes like that well. Better than me.'* He found himself on the verge of tears for the little girl and her family as well.

Outside the house, Marc talked to the officer again. "Any idea who did this?"

The cop responded, "Yeah, we apprehended him already. Some guy that lives around the corner. The girl gave us a description before you got here. Apparently he moved into the neighborhood a month or two ago and never registered with the sex offenders' list."

"Fucking monster," Brian muttered upon hearing the policeman's story.

As they began to drive away, the policeman ran towards the ambulance, waving at them. Marc rolled down his window and he told the medics "Can you drive around the corner and check him out? I just got a call over the radio that something's wrong with the perp."

"Oh great. Yeah, I guess so," answered Marc.

"So now we have to treat this asshole too?" Brian said disgustedly.

They pulled up to the next scene where several police cars were also parked. Brian walked up to one of the officers, saying, "Y'all have the perp of the signal forty-two around the corner?" referring to the rape by the police signal code, forty-two.

"Yeah, says he's having chest pains. We had to call you to check him out. He's in the car," the officer responded.

"Is he violent or anything?" Marc asked.

"No, just an asshole. We ran his record. Found out he got out of jail a month ago and he's been staying in his friend's house here."

"Got out of jail? For what?" Brian asked.

"Same thing. Sex offender. Got off on some technicality," he said.

As he opened the door, the smell of alcohol and the perpetrator's voice met their noses and ears. "I'm havin' a damn heart attack. I need to go to the hospital! I'm gonna sue your ass if you don't get me to the hospital!" screeched the man.

When they got him out of the car, Brian and Marc recognized him as the man they had picked up at the prison complex after being arrested for soliciting sex from a nine year-old. "Yes, indeed!" Marc said upon realizing who he was.

Brian's rage had returned. Only this time it was directed towards the man in handcuffs before him, not Marc. *This creep again! I can't believe it! Playing the same game as last time to try to get out of going to jail!'* Brian pictured the poor girl's blood trickling down her legs after this man's brutal crime. She shared the same name as his girlfriend Tammy, Tamara. Hatred boiled within him. He suddenly had a flashback to the dream he had almost forgotten. Brian envisioned the cowbirds picking ticks off the rhinoceros, and thought back to Marc's reasons for doing what he did. Through his rage at the perpetrator and sadness for Tamara and frustration at his own ineffectiveness, he had a moment of realization. He recalled Marc's words from two days before, which now seemed prophetic: *'When a rapist or child molester gets off scot-free on a legal technicality, is that right?'* Brian reached down and felt the man's pulse. As he felt his wrist, he caught Marc's eyes and looked meaningfully into them, and said "I think he may really be having a heart attack."

The policeman next to them looked shocked. Marc stared back at Brian. A look of perplexity crossed his face as Marc checked the man's pulse himself. *'Heart attack? His pulse feels fine! What is Brian saying?'* Then a moment later *'Is he telling me what I think he's telling me?'* Marc wondered. "Go ahead and take off the cuffs," Marc asked the officer while regarding Brian warily.

After removing the handcuffs, Marc held the man by the arm as they walked to the ambulance. The man kept on hollering at the cops "I'm dyin' here! I told you I was and y'all are sayin' I ain't having chest pains and sayin' I raped somebody! I'll sue all your asses!"

"Just get in," Marc ordered him. All three got into the truck. Brian instructed him to get on the stretcher; Marc closed the door. "They picked you up for assaulting that girl?"

Now out of earshot of the cops, the man spoke freely, much like the last time Brian and Marc had encountered him. "Yeah, so what? Who cares? She's just some little nigger bitch anyway. Plenty more where she came from. What they serving at the hospital for lunch?"

Brian and Marc looked at each other. The pure disgust on both their faces was evident. Brian finally said to Marc "You know, I think I'm beginning to understand."

Marc took a second to process Brian's words in his head. A look of relief mixed with apprehension crossed his countenance.

"I guess we should treat his heart attack," Brian offered.

"Yeah," said the man on the stretcher. "I'm dyin' here!"

"Yes," Marc responded to him. "We'll do all we can, sir."

Marc applied an oxygen cannula to his nostrils and Brian started an IV. Marc opened the bag of equipment and stared at the contents of the medicine inventory. He pulled out the spray bottle of Nitroglycerine. It worked by dilating the blood vessels, increasing blood flow to the heart but reducing blood pressure. Each spray had four hundred micrograms of nitroglycerine. A patient was never supposed to have more than three sprays at a time because it could severely drop blood pressure to dangerous levels. There was enough in the bottle for two hundred sprays. Marc pulled the sprayer off the bottle and handed it to Brian to give to the man. "Make sure you swallow the whole bottle," he instructed. "It will burn a bit in your mouth but it'll help with your chest pain."

Brian gave Marc a complimentary glance. *'Not bad!'* he thought. The man took the bottle from Brian. "Cheers!" he said drunkenly, downing the entire bottle in one gulp. "Whoo, you were right! That does burn! Fuck!"

Marc reached into the bag again and pulled out another medication, Cardizem. "You know how Cardizem works?" he asked Brian.

Brian recited from memory what he had learned from studying pharmacology for paramedic class. "It's a calcium channel blocker. Reduces blood pressure and heart rate by inhibiting the contractility of the heart and blood vessels."

"Very good," said Marc as he mixed the entire vial of one hundred milligrams with a syringe of saline solution. "Now how will this help our friend here?"

Brian pictured the man's blood vessels dilating from the gigantic Nitroglycerine overdose. Such an enormous dose would cause his blood vessels to almost completely relax, reducing his blood pressure to next to nothing, causing him to pass out from lack of circulation to the brain and heart. The Cardizem would increase that effect and reduce the pumping ability of the heart to nothing also. As Brian pictured the man's blood pooling inside his body, not circulating, his thoughts drifted to the blood pooling inside little Tamara's knickers from her ruined genitals.

"Oh man, I feel weird," the man said. My head is... killing me..." he said just before passing out on the stretcher. He was drenched in sweat, his skin pale from the relative hypovolemic shock he was experiencing from the Nitroglycerine.

"It'll... it will make things better," Brian replied to Marc's question. Marc drew up the entire one hundred milligrams into the syringe and handed it to Brian. The correct dose for anyone was a maximum of twenty milligrams. "He should probably get the whole thing, right?" Brian confirmed as he injected all the Cardizem into the IV line.

Marc and Brian had deliberately left off attaching the EKG monitor so that it wouldn't record what was surely a normal heart rhythm up until then. When they attached the leads and switched it on, it showed an extremely slow heartbeat, twenty-eight beats per minute. Marc printed a strip and watched as the Cardizem continued to take effect. The rate slowed to twenty, ten, then zero. The man on the stretcher was turning blue. "Guess it's time to intubate him," Marc said, handing Brian the airway equipment.

"I've never intubated anyone before." Brian looked nervous, but took the laryngoscope and placed it down the man's throat, peering inside. The membranes in his throat were pale, deprived of blood flow. Brian found the vocal cords and slipped the tube between them. He attached the Ambu bag and gave a few breaths as Marc listened to his chest to confirm placement of the tube. "You're in! Good job!" he congratulated Brian.

Brian reflexively continued to ventilate the man. Marc placed his hands on Brian's and removed them from the Ambu bag. "I know, it's habit," Brian said. "This feels weird, not doing CPR."

"What's the first drug you want to give?" Marc asked, his hand reaching into the bag.

"Let's see, he's in asystole. Epi!" Brian answered correctly. Brian had worked enough codes that he knew exactly what drugs to give for each heart arrhythmia.

"Good!" Marc said, smiling as he squirted the Epinephrine into the wheel well. "Next?"

"Atropine!" answered Brian as began to get the hang of Marc's *modus operandum*. Marc handed him the Atropine syringe and it followed the Epi into the wheel well.

Marc got out the carbon dioxide detector and placed it in his own mouth. "I guess I'm ready to go," he said, his words garbled by the plastic attachment he held in his mouth.

Brian gaped wide-eyed as he saw what Marc was doing with the CO2 detector. *'Brilliant! I would never have thought of that!'* he thought to himself. Giving Marc a nervous smile, he got out the truck to get into the front and drive. A cop met him, startling Brian.

"Well? How is he?" the officer inquired.

Brian fumbled on his words for a second, panicking in his head. *'Shit! What do I say? That I killed his disgusting ass? Fuck, think of something!'*

"Looks like he really had a heart attack. He just went into cardiac arrest," he answered the cop. *'Please, please believe that!'*

"Fuck!" exclaimed the cop. "That's gonna be a shitload of paperwork!"

"Are you gonna be in trouble? That happening to an arrestee?" Brian asked.

"I hope not. It'd be a huge shitstorm if I hadn't asked for the ambulance, though. Glad I did. Can't say I'm sorry to hear that happened to that scumbag," the cop answered.

"Well, okay, we'll be at University," Brian ended the conversation, glad he didn't seem suspiciously nervous. *'Hell, the cop's probably more nervous about it than I am!'* he realized.

He drove to the hospital with his siren going the entire time, even when there were no cars in front of him. *'Just because it's legal doesn't make it right - letting the parasites live,'* Brian remembered Marc saying. Now he understood. The rapist had gotten off from being imprisoned before. He likely knew how to do so again. Often, charges were never even filed on rape because the family and the victim didn't want to undergo the humiliation of reliving the events in a trial. If the scum in the back of the truck had gotten off again, who would his next victim be? He imagined the "beautiful chirren" that Joyce had said that he and his own Tamara would one day have. He pictured himself in the place of the weeping father he had seen today, his own little daughter raped, humiliated and bleeding from the assault of the man that now lay in the back of his truck. *'If the man who raped my own daughter was killed by the paramedics that brought him to the hospital, I'd kiss their feet.'*

Brian pulled up onto the ramp at University Hospital. Mignon St. Germain greeted them "Hey honey! We were having a good day till you brought us this!" she joked. "What ya got?" she asked as they rolled into the trauma room.

"He was under arrest, complaining of chest pain. We figured he was bullshitting to get out of going to jail but he was bradycardic and hypotensive on scene," Marc informed, pulling out the EKG printout of the heart rate of thirty. "He coded on scene, he's been in asystole ever since. he's had five Epi's, three Atropines, Bicarb, Narcan and Dextrose."

"Under arrest? For what?" asked Doctor Lovejoy.

"Raping an eight year-old." Brian said emotionlessly.

The ER staff took a collective breath for a second as they stared at the dead rapist on the table, then resumed working on the man. "Total down time?" the doctor asked.

Mark looked at his clipboard. "Twenty minutes."

"Okay, let's call it. Fifteen fifty-one," announced Dr. Lovejoy, stating the official time of death.

And that was it. Brian felt like there should have been some huge investigation by the ER staff into the cause of the man's death, but he realized he was just being paranoid. It was, after all, his first time eliminating a parasite from society. He cleaned the stretcher, trying to look as if nothing was wrong, but nervous to the point of nausea. After a few minutes of no divine lightning striking him and no FBI whooshing in to arrest him, he relaxed a little and thought to himself *'That was easy!'*

He jumped when Mignon came up behind him and put her hand on his back. "Hah hah! I startled you!" she said laughing.

"Hey, when you get off work at midnight, you wanna come have drinks with the rest of us? I asked Marc too; he's coming."

Brian relaxed. "Sure, that sounds great! I'll see you then!" *I could use a drink!*

Later, when Marc had finished writing his report, he met Brian at the truck and smoked. "Well, how do you feel?" Marc asked.

Brian thought for a while, wondering how to put his many emotions into words. At last he answered, "I feel like the world is a better place. But you were wrong about one thing."

"Oh?" Marc raised his eyebrows. "What's that?"

"Remember you said 'making the world a better place is never easy and seldom welcomed'?"

"Yes."

"It's not that hard."

Marc laughed heartily, saying "Brian, you really will make a great paramedic one day!"

Chapter 12

Marc and Brian went about the rest of their shift as if nothing unusual had happened, other than Brian feeling nervous and occasionally asking Marc about his "therapy." They were truly partners now, linked by more than just working in the same ambulance together.

"I take it you've never gotten caught?" asked Brian.

"No. Closest was when you kept asking about that dialysis code we had a few months ago. Yes, that was one of mine. The circumstances have to be absolutely perfect. Our friend the rapist was probably the riskiest one ever. Tell you what, let's not talk about this too much, okay?" Marc suggested.

"Good idea," Brian agreed.

They finished out their shift, transporting a female with abdominal pain, a male that had gotten beaten up, a man complaining of chest pain, and a woman that had passed out, "overheated," according to her friends, despite the forty degree temperature. Marc chose not to give the patient's friends a lesson on physics; they did not seem to be the type that would be interested in the laws of thermodynamics. It was more likely that the patient's heavy crack abuse and heart rate of a hundred and fifty may have had something to do with her complaint.

The rest of their shift was otherwise uneventful. When Brian went home, he again got little sleep as he pondered his role in the rapist's death, but he felt better than the night before for two reasons. For one, he now knew the truth about Marc and had begun to empathize with his reasons for doing what he did. Second, he considered his own part in what had transpired in the back of his ambulance. The rapist was not only a child predator, but one who manipulated the system to his own advantage specifically to subvert justice at Brian's own expense, as well as Marc's and the police he would try to evade by calling for the ambulance. He imagined how many real patients with legitimate medical problems had to wait for an ambulance while the rapist played his little game with EMS. He realized that his own tax dollars were being used to pay for the continuous abuse of the police, EMS and the hospital visits; the thought infuriated Brian, and he felt better that today, he and Marc really had made a difference in the world for the better.

The next day, Brian and Marc were both in a good mood. They had both had a moment that made them feel better about the world they lived in and sharing a moment like that with someone makes it all the more enjoyable. They didn't speak of the incident, but it occurred to each of them how perverse it was to enjoy their mutual feelings when they involved killing someone. *'I've enjoyed calls where someone was critically hurt or sick, or even died before; enjoying yourself at someone else's expense is part of the nature of this job,'* Brian thought to himself.

'Those are usually the best calls,' Marc also thought. *'Making a difference while there's death all around is why I became a paramedic in the first place.'*

Both medics chuckled a slightly evil laugh to themselves as they pondered the enjoyment they got at the rapist's expense.

"Stand by to copy," said Mandy over the radio. She gave them a call at Canal and Royal for a "female down."

"Oh God, who will this be?" Marc complained.

They pulled up to the corner they had been to so many times before for Aaron Sparrowhawk, David Spencer, Johannes Sunville, Deborah Gill and lots of their other frequent fliers. Down on the sidewalk near the liquor store was a woman that neither EMT recognized. Another woman, obviously drunk but talking constantly, sat next to her. The patient was passed out from the bottle of cheap gin next to her, soaked in urine.

"Y'all gonna take care o' her? She's my frien'. I called you when she pashed out," the other drunk woman slurred to them.

Marc put on a pair of gloves before he dug through her wet

pockets looking for any identification. "I hope it's her own urine, at least," he said as he withdrew some sodden paperwork from her pants.

"Let's see... Discharge paperwork from two hospital visits, one yesterday, one from two days ago," he said as he unfolded the yellow sheets of paper and read them. "Both say 'diagnosis: acute alcohol intoxication.' Discharge instructions: 'Stop drinking.' Looks like our princess here is a little non-compliant with her discharge instructions. Oh, and there's one more paper here, a court summons. Can you guess what for?" he asked Brian.

Brian laughed a little, "Oh this a tough one. But I'll just take a stab at it... public intoxication?"

"Very good! You win the bonus round!" Marc joked back. He read the name off the papers. "Ronnie Ritchie? Is that you?" he shouted at the woman while rubbing his knuckles on her sternum to wake her up.

"Ow, damn it!" she shouted back at him, jumping slightly from her sidewalk stupor. "Yeah," she answered and laid back down on the pavement.

"She jusht got in town lasht week from Chicago. I been keepin' her company, bein' all new in town and all," the drunk friend offered.

"She's only been in town for a week and she's already been arrested and gone to the hospital twice for being passed out drunk?" Brian marveled. "What did she come to New Orleans for?"

"She didn't have nothin' else to do. Y'all don't have to take her to the hospilal," slurred the friend. "I jusht wanted you to make sure she's okay." She was very near passing out herself, barely able to sit up straight, her dirty, stringy blond hair almost completely covering her face.

Marc and Brian couldn't leave her to sleep it off. "If she decided to get up and stumble into traffic or fall and hurt herself, somehow we'd be the ones liable for it," Brian explained to the friend. "You set the wheels into motion when you called us, and we can't leave her like this."

Upon realizing that the ambulance crew was going to take her friend away, she picked up the gin bottle from off the sidewalk and began to slug back the remnants of it. Brian pulled the bottle out of her hand and emptied it out into the gutter, saying "Why don't you get up the street and go home yourself? You look like you've had enough yourself."

Marc had fetched the stretcher and he and Brian lifted Ronnie onto it. As they fastened the safety belts around her, a fresh puddle of urine pooled between her legs. "Fabulous," Brian commented as he considered the task of cleaning the stretcher at the hospital. "I guess this'll be a new frequent flier. We get rid of one abscess on the ass of humanity, and immediately there's a new one to take their place."

"I think there's a waiting list," Marc said. "It's a never-ending cycle."

At the hospital, Brian scrubbed the stretcher clean and Marc smoked as they waited for their next call. Mandy called them over the radio, "Copy a phone number."

Marc jotted down the phone number on his clipboard and keyed up his radio, "Ten-four. Who am I calling?"

"It's the coroner's office," Mandy replied.

Brian and Marc stared at each other, panicky looks overtaking both their faces. "Oh shit," Brian said.

Marc pulled out his cell phone and dialed, taking a deep breath. It rang on the other end for an agonizing ten seconds. "Hello?" whomever it was at the coroner's office answered.

"Um, hi. This is Marcus DeSalle with New Orleans EMS. I was asked to call this number."

"Oh, thanks Mister DeSalle. This is Evan Thompson with Orleans Parish Coroner's Office. I'm a death investigator. You picked up a Raymond Naquin yesterday? He was under arrest with NOPD and died in their custody."

"Yes, sir, I think that was his name," Marc replied as evenly as he could as he waited for the death investigator to mention some damning evidence against him.

"Well, of course there has to be an investigation whenever an arrestee dies; I'm in the process of doing that. Can you give me some details about the call?" Thompson asked.

Marc moved the phone away and whispered to Brian, "It's about our guy yesterday!" Brian's eyes got even more panicky as his fear was confirmed.

"Um, well, he was complaining of chest pains when we got to the scene," Marc began, trying to not sound worried over the phone. "At first, my partner and I thought he was bullshitting us just to try to get out of being arrested, but when we put him on the EKG monitor, we saw that his heart rate was about thirty. A few minutes later it dropped down to nothing and we started CPR and worked him all the way to the hospital." Marc tried to give as few details as he could. "Did... um, did the autopsy show anything?"

"Well that's the thing," Thompson responded. Marc closed his eyes and waited for the hammer to fall.

"The autopsy showed some heart disease, but not a heart attack. There was no specific infarct in his heart. He had some liver damage, consistent with a history of alcoholism, but not really enough to kill someone. There wasn't any trauma so it's not like the cops roughed him up or anything. Toxicology report showed alcohol and marijuana, but not enough to kill him either."

Marc offered nothing; he merely replied "Hmm, that's strange. We worked him like we would any other cardiac arrest."

"Yes, I have your report right here. Looks like you did a good job." Marc took a breath, feeling like it was his first breath in years. "Can you tell me anything that might have happened? Did Naquin tell you anything that might shed some light?" Thompson inquired.

'Boy, could I!' Marc pondered.

"No, he just said his chest hurt. I picked him up a few months ago when he was under arrest before and he was complaining of chest pain then too, but I couldn't find anything wrong with him. We just took him to the hospital and followed the usual protocol for chest pain - oxygen, IV, aspirin and

123

nitroglycerine," Marc said.

"Yes, I was reading his arrest records," said Thompson. "He was quite a winner. Four arrests for child molestation, one conviction. Spent four years in Angola for that one. A couple more for failure to register as a sex offender, some for public drunkenness, theft, indecent exposure, trespassing. Nineteen arrests in all. It seems that he went to the hospital upon all of his last seven arrests. The cops called for EMS each time."

"Yes, like I said, I picked him up one of those times. I figured he was just trying to get out of being arrested, but we still have to treat him. Do you think that he had some underlying problem that no one ever picked up on?" Marc suggested, hoping his idea would fly with the investigator.

"Hm. I suppose so. That's the only thing I could think of too," he said.

"Yeah, I can't think of anything else either. Maybe the combination of his chronic problems and whatever else he had going on was what did him in," Marc offered what he hoped would sound like a clinical analysis, trying to curry Thompson's favor.

"I've pretty much exhausted any other means of death, without shooting in the dark for some weird diagnosis. Judging from this guy's history, I don't think anyone will miss him too much anyway. My report will just say he died of natural causes. Thanks for your time. You keep safe out there," he finished.

"Thanks, you too!" Marc bid him, hanging up his phone. "Whew!" he sighed to Brian who had been hanging onto every word of Marc's conversation.

"Well? What?" Brian asked, almost hysterical with anxiety.

Marc cast him a long look, relief evident in his expression. "Natural causes."

"Oh Jesus! Thank God! I almost shit myself!" Brian replied, finally relaxing in his seat.

"No kidding! That death investigator seemed to think no one would miss such a scumbag, either," Marc commented.

Both sat in their seats, quietly contemplating their fate had any evidence been found implicating them. Marc had thought about it many times, of course, but this was the first time he actually had to speak to the coroner's office to lie about his actions.

After a few minutes, Brian spoke up, "Marc, I think it may be time to reconsider this. I know that it feels good, even right, to put these shitbags out of our misery, but that was just way too close."

Marc paused for a second before replying. "You know, I was just thinking the same thing. Getting rid of them doesn't really get rid of them. That's obvious, like our new shitbag, Ms. Ritchie, demonstrated this morning. It's not worth going to jail, or getting my own dose of potassium chloride for doing the world a favor."

Brian nodded meaningfully, but thought to himself *'He didn't actually say he would stop killing people, only that he was thinking about it and that it's not worth jail. But I've done enough with this. I'll just take that as a "yes" and shut the fuck up about it."*

"Good idea," he said to Marc. After a minute, Brian turned to Marc and asked "By the way, how did you get started on this crusade to get rid of the people causing all our social ills?"

Marc laughed, thinking back to a long time before. "How much time do you have? That, my friend, is a whole other story."

Glossary of Terms

Albuterol: A drug used to relieve wheezing and shortness of breath due to asthma, bronchitis or emphysema. Often given along with Atrovent.

Ambu bag: A manually squeezed device used to artificially breathe for a non-breathing patient.

Anoxia: Deprivation of oxygen to the body's tissues.

Artifact: Extraneous waves on an EKG printout caused by movement or electrical interference.

Arrhythmia: A general term describing any irregular or dangerous heart rhythm.

Asystole: A lack of any electrical activity in the heart, indicating death. "Flatlined."

Atropine: A drug used to treat a slow or absent heartbeat. (Also used for organophosphate poisoning, glaucoma and used to dilate pupils, though not in this book.)

Atrovent: Trade name for ipratropium bromide. A drug used to relieve wheezing and shortness of breath due to asthma, bronchitis or emphysema. Usually given in conjunction with

Albuterol.

Bicarb: Short for Sodium Bicarbonate, a drug used to treat low pH, which commonly occurs during cardiac arrest.

Bolus: A single administration of a large quantity of a drug.

Code: Medical slang for cardiac arrest.

D50: Short for D50W, Dextrose 50% in Water. A drug used to increase blood glucose (sugar) levels.

Defibrillation: An electrical shock administered to attempt to correct ventricular fibrillation.

Dextrose: A simple sugar in intravenous form used to treat low blood glucose (or "diabetic coma").

Dialysis: An artificial process to filter the blood and remove excess fluid when the kidneys have stopped functioning. Chronic dialysis patients usually have the procedure three times a week.

EMT: Abbreviation of Emergency Medical Technician. In this book, three levels of EMT are mentioned: Basic, Intermediate and Paramedic. Paramedics have the highest level of training and the greatest scope of practice.

Epinephrine: A drug used to treat allergic reactions, certain arrhythmias or extremely low blood pressure. Also called Adrenaline and "Epi." Generally supplied in two concentrations: 1:1,000 (highly concentrated) for subcutaneous or intramuscular injection and 1:10,000 (diluted) for intravenous administration.

ER: Emergency Room

ET: Abbreviation for Endotracheal, meaning "within the trachea," or windpipe.

FNG: Fucking New Guy

GCS: Abbreviation of Glasgow Coma Scale, used to measure the functionality of brain-injured patients. A normal GCS is 15.

ICU: Intensive Care Unit (of a hospital).

Intubate: The act of inserting an ET tube to establish an airway so as to artificially breathe for a patient.

IO: Abbreviation for Intraosseous; a type of needle to gain access to the bloodstream by being inserted into a bone rather than a vein.

JVD: Abbreviation for Jugular Vein Distention, enlargement of the veins in the neck.

Laryngoscope: An instrument used to visualize a patient's airway and vocal cords. Usually used for the placement of an ET tube.

MI: Abbreviation for Myocardial Infarction; a heart attack.

Narcan: A drug used to reverse the effects of opiates such as heroine or morphine. Also called Naloxone.

Neutral ground: A colloquial New Orleans term meaning the grassy median dividing a street.

PE: Abbreviation for Pulmonary Embolism, a blood clot or other body which blocks bloodflow to the lungs resulting in the inability to exchange oxygen and carbon dioxide.

Postictal: The period of confusion following a seizure.

Pneumo: Short for pneumothorax; a collapsed lung due to air, blood or fluid in the chest cavity. A tension pneumothorax inhibits breathing to a dangerous degree.

Pulseox: A device that measures the percentage of oxygen saturating the blood. Normal is 95-100%.

SIDS: Abbreviation for Sudden Infant Death Syndrome.

Signal 29: Police radio code for a death

Signal 42: Police radio code for a rape.

Sinus Bradycardia: A normally conducted heart rhythm at a rate of fewer than 60 beats per minute. Also called "Sinus Brady."

Sinus tach: Short for Sinus Tachycardia; a normally conducted heart rhythm at a rate between 100 and 150 beats per minute.

Tech: The act of caring for the patient alone in the back of the ambulance.

Thiamine: Vitamin B1.

Valium: A drug used to sedate or treat seizures.

Versed: A drug used for sedation.

Ventricular fibrillation: An arrhythmia with no organized electrical activity in the heart that generates no heartbeat, but which is treatable with medications and electrical shock. Also called "v-fib."

About the Author:

Born in 1965, Sean Fitzmorris is a native of New Orleans, Louisiana. He has worked at New Orleans' Emergency Medical Services at every level of EMT certification. He remains a Nationally Registered Paramedic. He has also been a Registered Nurse since 2005, specializing in Emergency and Critical care.

Found Wanting is Sean's first novel. He has worked as staff writer & editor for *Liquid* magazine in New Orleans as well as a freelance writer for *Best of New Orleans* magazine. In addition, he's written numerous travel articles for BootsnAll.com and Hostelworld.com.

Wondering how Marc got started on his deadly quest to eliminate the "parasites of society"? Keep watching for Weighed in the Balances, the prequel to this novel!

Connect with Sean!

Twitter: http://twitter.com/seanhfitz

Read his blog, "BurningTiger - Reborn!"

http://newburningtiger.blogspot.com

Made in the USA
Lexington, KY
03 January 2014